A

SAI SHRUTHI

Contents

Contents

Preface

I started writing this book as a hobby, as I was pursuing my studies. Didn't really expect that I would complete it. But I realized I was really into it. So, I did my best to bring out an engaging story for all of you out there.

This book is a work of interest and not that of a professional. I am neither a professional writer nor an English major. And this is my very first book. So, I sincerely hope you enjoy the book. I would like to thank you in advance.

Now... let's dive right into it!

Acknowledgements

First, I would like to thank myself. Because, if it wasn't for me, I wouldn't have been able to finish this book.

Just kidding! (Not really...)

I would like to thank everyone who reached this far because that would mean you read the book till the end and hopefully enjoyed it. Thanks for the support and your time.

Hope to meet you all again via my next book.

Contact info: saisruthikarthi@gmail.com

Prologue

'I don't want to live, nor do I want to die.
I want to flee. Away from all of this, where it is just me and me alone.
That could make it a lot easier and worth living.'

Not a day goes by without me having this thought. Almost every minute of every day, this is what I keep telling myself. It has been years now and I am still where I am with all those thoughts just enhancing each day, leading me to something I don't want to be doing.

There are times when I ask myself if I really deserve this. If I am fated to suffer this way. But then, the next question pops up, and the whole thought takes a different turn.

Am I even suffering?

I have parents. Guardians, per se. I have a roof over my head. I am quite educated if not much. I have a life a little better than the poor. There are people suffering for real, with real crappy problems and here I am complaining and arguing about a life that isn't as bad as the others. I should be here thanking God for this life but all I do is try to get away from this it.

Then why do I feel this way?

I heard somewhere, (or probably read somewhere) that everyone has their own problem and suffering. It could be a minor problem or could be a huge pain-in-the-ass problem. One's problem, whether small or big, cannot and *should not* be compared.

The human brain works differently among different people. The mind can calculate, figure out, and compare the problem we have with other people. In that sense, the mind tries to tell us and ease us with the fact that our problems are nothing but bullshit. It has us questioning ourselves and whether we are overthinking all the crap in our lives. We get stuck between trying to be happy and trying not to think about all the things we thought were just minor. But it doesn't really work, believe me!

And the reason is simple. Turns out, the mind isn't the only puppet master. The *heart* has its own mind and screws with us just as much as the brain.

Apparently, the heart doesn't just take commands from the mind. It has its own way of communicating and making us feel strange things. Although the mind is the powerhouse of the body that allows us to think, feel, and act, it's the heart that aches for all the decisions we end up making. The thoughts flowing in our head is also connected to our hearts. No matter what the thoughts are, it hurts the heart first, and eventually, the mind gives in. Since the heart and the mind are intimately connected, it's hard to choose between those two.

Some say we should follow the heart and some think that it's the mind that makes the right decisions.

I honestly don't know anymore. I have reached a point where any decisions I make or steps I take are eventually going to end up in a ditch.

So, I think it's quite clear what I am trying to say.

Or not. Whatever.

My life was a series of misery.

Until it wasn't...

1

Lily

Present day

"I swear dad! My friends are crushing on you. I mean, it is so weird for me. It's better if mom drops me at school from now on."

"Lily, sweetheart? You should show off this fact about your father rather than hide it," he says, winking at me.

"Gross, Jamie!" Mom points out. It makes me chuckle.

"Well honey, this is New York, and this kind of thing is very common here," he says to my mom with a smirk.

She mocks him and sticks out her tongue which makes him chortle.

My mom is *the* best human I have ever met. Of course, my dad is the best too but, if I had to prioritize, I'd go for my mom. She is literally my guardian angel. My best friend and my partner in crime. I sometimes wonder if this is even real. I mean, I hear a lot of complaints from my friends about their mothers, and when I deny those facts when it comes to my mom, they look at me all flustered. They never believed me. So, I had to invite them for dinner and let them hang out with my parents, especially my mother.

Since then, all my friends started to envy me. Not a day goes by when they don't mention my parents. They drop by my house at times to hang out with us. And as I mentioned earlier, a few of my friends started having a crush on my dad. Even thinking about it makes me want to barf.

But in all fairness, my dad *is* a heartthrob. And my mom? Well, she is the definition of *beauty*. My parents are the perfect match for each other. And I am probably the luckiest on earth to have been born to them.

"Honey?" my mom calls. That's when I realize I have been staring into nothingness during my bout of self-reflection. I snap out of it and notice my parents staring at me.

"I'll drop you off today. You okay, by the way?" My mom asks. The next thing I know, I am hugging my parents so tight, that I can feel them getting concerned.

I pull away and say, "There is nothing in this world that would make me love you guys any less. Thank you so much for bringing me into this world. I am so lucky to be your daughter."

They both smile and my dad goes, "You are just like your mother. Melodramatic, cliché, and perfect." My mom elbows him by the side with a laugh. He then kisses me on the forehead and says, "We love you too, sweetheart."

"Okay hon, come on it's getting late," my mom says and rushes towards the door but then stops midway to hug me and kiss me on the cheek. "You are *the* blessing I and Jamie were wishing for. So, thank *you* for being born to us," she says, with a huge smile on her face.

That right there is the reason why I am the happiest person on this planet.

~~~

"Pick you up at four?" My mom asks as I get off the car.

"Mom, I am actually going to Kelly's house after school. Will be back for dinner."

"Okay then. Don't be late. Have fun," she waves at me and takes off. I stand where I am until I see her car turn and disappear. I walk to my class and, I feel a hand lay on my shoulder. "Hey, girl!"

"Hey, Kelly." She is my next best friend, after my mom. Although, I never had to share anything with her that I haven't already told my mom. Whatever she knows, my mom knows. And sometimes my dad too. We have been friends since fourth grade and have never been apart. She is basically my sister. At least that's what my parents say whenever she comes home. A few years back I remember my mom telling her these exact words, "You are like my second daughter, Kelly. The bond you two have is so great. I sincerely hope you two stay like this forever." And then she gave her a pink dress that she bought for her when we were shopping. It was the same one as mine, except mine was lilac. She thought it would be cute if we wore it together so that it would look like we were sisters, and we do everything together. It was cute. Although I thought it was too childish, Kelly really loved it and apparently, now she loves *my* mom more than *her* mom. Not sure if it's okay but if she feels that way, so be it."

What's with the happy mood?" I ask.

"I am just excited for this evening. Listen, I have invited quite a few gangs. And by that, I mean, *boys*," she emphasizes on the word boys as if it's a magic word.

"So, we are the only girls then?"

"Yep," she says giggling with excitement.

"Are you serious? Kelly, we can't be the only two girls among a bunch of boys! Please tell me you are joking."

She gives me a familiar side look which interprets that she was messing with me. I let out a sigh of relief.

"Oh, and the basketball team is coming too."

At that, the relief just automatically vanishes. The school's basketball team is basically a bunch of breath-taking guys from the entire school. It's like all the handsome ones were chosen for the team, irrespective of their talent, which I hope is not the case. But it is so annoyingly true that the entire school, including a few guys, is all about them. The team did this, the team did that, the team...the team...THE TEAM!

I am like, enough already.

But all this comes to a halt and starts making sense when I am in the presence of Gavin Rickson. The team captain and not to mention, brutally attractive.

He is the only one to make me think about all the stuff, that makes the entire school think about the team. And by the team, I mean the *guys* on the team.

I have had a crush on him for over a year and a half and he obviously has no clue. I mean, we haven't even talked since they won the last basketball tournament, and I congratulated him. And by him, I mean the entire team, so it wasn't really a one-on-one conversation.

We did share a look a time or two. When he came down the hallway, wearing his basketball jersey, he gave me this look while tossing the ball from one hand to the other and that was so invading that I flinched. Both times. But I don't think it was intentional. Maybe he was looking for someone else, perhaps his girlfriend, and accidentally laid his eyes on me. Or he was probably just looking around as he was walking and happened to see me since I was in his way of staring at things. Either way, I felt things when he looked at me and it was scorching.

I am snapped out of my thoughts when the teacher calls out my name. I didn't even realize I was seated inside the classroom.

"Are you still with us, Miss Brooks?" He asks.

"Yes, Mr. Hudson. Sorry about that." And then, I go back to feeling nervous thinking about how I would manage to be in the same place as Gavin for more than seconds.

I am so glad we don't share the same classes. He has such a distracting face which would make it hard for me to concentrate. I mean right now, he is not even in the class, and I am being distracted by him. There is no way I would even graduate with him in the same room as me.

~~~

Kelly did a lot of work to make this party thing look wild. It's such a weird look now that her parents are out. The whole place looks like a bachelor's apartment with nothing but drinks and pizzas. And by drinks, I mean soda. A few guys and two other girls are out in the front yard having drinks and chit-chatting. As we are waiting for the rest of them to show up, I get a text from dad.

Dad: Lily, we are going out for groceries. We've left the keys under the mat just in case you come early. Also, do you want anything?

I check my bag for the keys I usually carry. But it's not there. The fact that I forgot my keys today, which is so rare, feels odd. Things have been weird today for some reason. Or maybe it's just the fact that am going to see Gavin in a few minutes and it's making me feel weird and apparently, the universe has been giving me signs since this morning which now makes sense. Forgetting the keys, getting yelled at in class for the first time, and to top all that, a weird feeling.

Me: Maybe some ice cream.

I am definitely going to need some ice cream tonight.

Dad: Done. See you tonight.

Me: Okay dad. XO.

I hear a car pulling over and stiffen as soon as I see him get off. I hate how he makes me feel without even realizing it.

He makes his way through the guys and looks at me and then immediately looks away. That stare lasted at least two seconds and two seconds is a lot when it comes to eye contact. That definitely wasn't just a 'looking around' look. It was as if he was looking *for* me. Again, I could be delusional, so never mind me.

I go back into her kitchen to grab a soda. I see a few people I recognize but I have never talked to them, so I just move past them. When I come back into the living room, I see two people making out. At first, I don't get a good glance at their faces but when I do, I go into shock and almost drop the soda off my hand.

It's the two people I never thought I would see, doing what they are doing. I could not digest the fact that my best friend ended up kissing the *only* guy I have ever liked. I storm out of there so fast, that no one really notices my tears as I walk out of her house, to the street.

I rush back home but only to remember that my parents are out. God, I wanted to talk to my mom so badly. This is the first time I am upset with her for not being here right now when I need her, even though it's not her fault.

I go into my bedroom, unlock the door, and lay on the bed on my stomach, hugging a pillow. I take my phone and start texting my mom.

Me: !!!!!!!!!!!!!!!!!!!!!!!!!!!!!

This is our secret code for when something serious or dangerous happens. At first, I thought this was too silly and easy but it kind of makes sense now. The greater the number of exclamatory marks, the more intense the feeling. My mom told me to use this in any situation I feel uncomfortable, scared, or lonely and she would come no matter what it was without any question. She takes it pretty seriously, so I have never used it for small issues. This is the first time I am using it. I think only we both know about the code. Am not even sure if my dad knows it.

I check their location to see if they are anywhere near home. We all have the app to track each other, and we don't find it weird or offensive. Just as I scroll through the directions, I get a text from my mom.

Mom: Be right there, hon.

At that, I roll back and stare at the ceiling with tearful eyes, waiting for them to reach home.

2
Sarah

Way back then...

I have never felt the need to celebrate birthdays. In fact, I hate birthdays. Especially mine. Because there is nothing to be happy about it. I should not have been born. My own parents thought that. Which is why they abandoned me right after I was born. Or maybe they both died right after knowing they gave birth to a girl.

Nah. I am pretty sure it's the first one. They can always make babies. If not this one, the next one. And if not that, then another again, and so on. It makes sense though. Being born as a girl in an Indian family even at good times can be devastating.

But what I don't understand is, why would they abandon me if I was not born *in* India. I have heard of parents killing their daughters right after they are born or abandoning them after their birth in India. Apparently, it's common in India to kill girl children. Although I am not sure if that's the case now. Thanks to my parents who abandoned me, I have never been to India, and I probably never will.

The point is, I was born in the USA. And yet, I was abandoned. Maybe there was some other reason but all I could think of is the fact that I am a girl. I will never know the answer. I have never seen them. I don't know how they look or their names or their whereabouts. Not that I care. I definitely hate them from the bottom of my heart. Even if I get to meet them, I will not give them the satisfaction of knowing the daughter they so carelessly and mercilessly abandoned. How could parents do that to an infant? Again, it's going to be unanswered.

Anyway, two or three years after I was abandoned, I was adopted by a couple. It was surprising that they adopted an Indian girl child. Although, I was not mature enough to know any of those things. I was three years old. I could only understand and speak much. I thought they were my real parents, and they came back for me after a really long trip. At least that's what I was told. I grew up in a big mansion-type of house with huge stairs and wood floors. It was great to finally be in a place I could call home. And the best part, I had a mom and a dad.

Years passed. I was happy. I was living. I went to school, made a few friends, and had the time of my life.

"Are you excited about your birthday party, dear?" My mother asked.

"Yes, mom. I can't wait for my friends to show up for my party," I said, with a little excitement.

"I can't believe you are turning eight already," my father said.

I don't know why I remember it so vividly. It was one of the few things I remember from that young age.

"I know. Our girl seems to be growing so fast," my mother said, with a smile. Then there was a knock on the door. I jumped with joy hoping it was my friends. But it was someone who came for my father. He was asked to meet his clients for some urgent business.

That's right. I was mature enough to know what a business meant.

"Mr. Richard, they are expecting you. They won't have a deal unless you show up," the man said.

"Alright. Give me a minute," my father said and grabbed his briefcase. He then whispered, "Happy birthday, Sarah," into my ears and took off.

That made me sad. I wanted my father to be at the party. I wanted everyone at my party. And just like that, the joy in me vanished. And since none of my friends showed up, I was no longer interested. I went up to my room and sobbed.

It was the worst birthday that I have ever known and that's why I hate it now. My mother never bothered to come up and check on me. I was kind of waiting for her to walk through that door and console, but she never did. I went down to see if she was still there, but she wasn't. But the maid was still in the kitchen. When she saw me, she had a huge smile on her face. She called me and fed me my birthday cake.

"Come here, sweetheart," she called. "Here, have this. I got you a present."

"Thank you, Aunty Rose," I said and started unwrapping the gift. It was a cute little hairpin with a pink flower on it. That made me smile. I loved it. "Thank you so much, Aunty Rose," I said and hugged her tight. The realization that my parents never gifted me anything on my birthday hit me so hard, that I had to hide the pretty hairpin Aunty Rose gave me. I was not mad at my parents for not gifting me anything though. I was eight. Nothing much mattered more than their love for me but even that seemed too far at that point. It was devastating as a kid.

"Listen, dear. Your parents are probably tired. You should go get some sleep yourself. Shall I tuck you in, real quick?" She asked in her sweet, soft tone.

"Okay," I said and nodded at the same time. She took off her apron and carried me to my room and tucked me perfectly. My parents never did that. She was a better parent than both of my parents combined.

"Good night, sweetheart. See you tomorrow," she said and tucked my hair behind my ear, with a smile on her face.

"I love you, Aunty Rose," I said. She didn't respond for a few seconds, but I could see the tears in her eyes.

"Aw thank you, dear. Aunty Rose loves you too," she said, kissing my forehead, and left the room.

I always liked her. She was my first friend ever. Her name was Rosie and I used to call her Aunty Rose. Actually, she was the only one to not make me feel unwanted. At times, my parents made me feel unwanted and worthless. Although I was a kid, I could sense the hatred. I was not sure why they felt that way about me though. They would change their attitudes toward me from time to time. I never understood why. I always thought maybe I did something wrong, so I would go and apologize to them. But still, nothing. All those times when I felt down, Aunty Rose was there for me. She would cheer me up, make cookies for me, and even help me sleep at times. She was my all-time go-to person until she wasn't. We left the mansion house in less than a year and rented an even smaller house since my father's so-called business went down and he lost all the money. He had to sell the house to pay his business partners and the bank. We could not afford all the things we used to. Thus, the small house and no maid. I remember crying for weeks because I missed Aunty Rose so much. I would ask my parents if we could call her and meet her. They always refused and lashed at me.

Crying became a daily routine for me. I cried for no reason at all. I was messed up. All the happy times and memories were replaced by all the worse and hurtful things done to me. Getting yelled at for no reason, getting beaten up for no reason, working, and doing house chores like a maid. I was only ten and I was maxed out with stress and not knowing what to do.

The other day, I was in the backyard, drying clothes when I heard my mother call me. "Sarah! Come here at once."

I rushed back in to see her on the couch, reading a book with her leg propped on the coffee table at the front.

"Yes, mother?"

"Could you bring me my glasses? It's on the desk in my room," she said in a calm tone, which I hadn't heard in a long time. So, I was kind of relieved and happy that my mother was finally talking to me casually even though she was acting like a total bitch.

"Here, mother," I said, handing her the glasses.

"Thank you. You may go now."

She never looked at my face during our little conversation, but I still felt it was the best conversation I had with my mother in a long time. I was happy that day.

I went back to continue my work and smiled the entire time I did it. I never knew a small, meaningless conversation could make someone this happy. I thought everything could go back to normal.

I looked up at the sky. It was blue.

I looked at the clothes I was drying. It was dirt-less and white.

I looked back at my home. It was, finally, a happy home for me.

At least that's what I thought it was.

Silly me.

3

Jamie

Back then...

I saw her, sipping her lonely coffee on a lonely bench behind our college building. It was the third time I saw her, all alone and probably sad. I don't think she noticed me. All three times.

I saw her up close only once when I walked past her the second time. She is never aware of the things happening around her. Or at least that's what I thought from what I had observed. All three times. She always stared at her coffee cup and the notes or paper in front of her. After every sip, she wrote something. Probably to someone. Perhaps her boyfriend.

Because from the looks of it, there was no way she could've been single. She was so gorgeous with beautiful, wavy brunette hair.

She didn't look American. And most importantly, she was sad. Which made her look way more beautiful. If that was even possible.

However, according to her expressions and the fact that she looked sad, she probably must have been heartbroken. I wanted to punch the guy who made her feel this miserable. Or whoever it was, the reason for her misery. But I still couldn't get over the fact that she was so beautiful no matter how she was.

I felt her gaze on me. She was probably looking at me.

'*Shoot. She is looking at me.*'

I didn't realize I was staring at her the entire time I was contemplating.

'*Now I must look like a creep to her. Great. Now she is smiling at me.*

Wait.

She is *smiling* at me.

Smiling at me!'

Damn, she was beautiful as hell when she smiled. No scratch that. She was beautiful as *heaven* when she smiled. Although, I don't really know what heaven looked like. It probably looked like her smile, her eyes, and her *heart*.

I know I just met her, but I thought I knew her. She waved her hand and left. She didn't wait for me to respond. I looked around to make sure that the smile and the wave were intended for me. I saw a few girls making their way toward the path she just took. Maybe she waved at them. But she left. Which could mean she was probably waving me bye before leaving.

'*Great! Now I am blabbering to myself like an idiot. God, I haven't even met her up close to talk to her properly and she already makes me feel this way.*'

I have never in my life, felt that way. Until now, of course.

'That woman was going to be my demise.

Or yet, better.

She could be my *paradise.*'

I wished for the latter...

4

Lily

Present day

I hear my parents' car pulling over. *Thank God!* I have been self-deprecating since I came home. I would have reached my limit if they hadn't come any sooner.

"Sweetie? You upstairs?" Dad calls out. "Here is your ice cream. It's your favourite flavour."

Just as I reach to open my bedroom door, I get a call. I look at the screen and my anger and tears find their way back to me. I can't talk to her. At least not right now. I toss my phone on the bed and head downstairs.

My dad had already helped himself with the ice cream he bought me. And butterscotch with chocolate chips just so happens to be my father's favourite flavour as well. I don't mind though. That's a big bucket of ice cream and I am pretty sure he won't be able to have it all by himself. I head toward my dad, and he feeds me a spoonful of ice cream. I sit next to him and grab the spoon from him. Because now that I have had a taste of it, I can't let go. I crave more. "Where is mom?" I ask mouthful. He nods his head in the direction of their room.

"You know you can talk to me too, right?" He says in a calm tone, but I feel a little bad. Because it is true. I *can* talk to him. About anything. He is such a cool, awesome human. "Of course, dad. I know," I say as I stick the spoon in the ice cream bucket and slide it to him. He goes for the spoon when I say, "I like this guy from school. Well, a crush if you will. But I have never talked to him. He is so cool. He is the captain of the basketball team," I say, looking at him. He gives me a witty smile. Then he takes another spoonful. Before eating it, he says, "So, you like him, but you haven't told him and now he is with someone else. Is that it?" He has the spoon in his mouth now and is looking at me. He clearly gets my facial expressions, so he speaks before I even say or ask anything. "I was once your age, Lil."

That's right. Duh.

"So, who was the girl?" He asked taking another spoonful.

"Kelly," I say without looking at him. But I could see him pause his hand with the spoonful of ice cream mid-air from the corner of my eye. I turn to look at him and he is like, "Our Kelly?"

I nod. The fact that my dad just said "Our Kelly" makes it even harder for me now. He doesn't speak for a few seconds. I get it though. I wouldn't be able to come up with anything to back that up. Hell, I stormed out of that sight. So, yeah.

"I saw them making out today," I say, breaking the silence. "I didn't know they were a thing."

"So, she knew you liked him and still did what she did?"

I don't answer that, but my silence answers my dad's question. He makes a face to let me know that it's not her fault. "Okay, fine. I never told her. I never told anyone. Not even to you guys. Well, until now."

"Sweetheart," he cups his hands on either side of my face and says, "She is your best friend. If she knew you liked that guy, she would never have started anything with him, and you know it." I do know that. She would never do such a thing. Ever. "But now, it's too late. She is his girlfriend now and you should respect that and move on." He is right.

Ugh. I hate that my dad is right. But most of all, I feel so good talking to him. This is the first time I have ever shared anything this serious with him first. It's usually mom and then dad. That makes me think about how my dad must have felt. Even though I did share stuff with him, he was never the first receiver. But he never said anything or showed any kind of disapproval. I go to mom all the time because it has been like that since I was a kid. She is the first person I see when I wake up, the first person I see after I come home from school. So, it was natural that I went to my mom first for everything. But now, after this conversation with my dad, I realized I don't have to rely on my mother alone. Even though I already knew that I never considered it. But now, I feel so good after sharing this with my dad. Just as good as I would feel with my mom. The realization hit me so hard.

Both mom *and* dad are my saviours. Always will be.

"Thanks, Dad," I say and hug him. He hugs me back with such appreciation that I could feel he is so glad I talked to him.

Just as I pull away from my dad, I see my mom standing in the doorway with her shoulder leaning on the door frame. Her arms are crossed over her chest, and she is smiling at us. We both stare at her but then her gaze moves to my dad. When I look at him, he smiles too. I am confused and clearly left out of whatever they are doing. I give out a sigh and say, "What is happening?" I look from my mom to my dad and raise both my hands in the air. "Well?"

"Your dad wanted to talk to you this time. When you texted me, I told him what it meant. He was curious and eager to talk to you. He wanted to be a part of whatever you were going through. So, I let him do it this time. I guess you can use that code with him as well now," my mom says as she tucks a strand of my hair behind my ear. Besides, even *I* wanted him to talk to you. Your father is way better at talking than me. See how he managed to make you smile just now. If it were me, you would have listened to me talk nonsense until you felt better. He did it in a matter of minutes," she says, playfully tousling his hair. I am grateful she did what she did. I got to talk to my dad about my feelings thanks to her. Now I can talk to either of them anytime, any day.

"You guys are so cool." They both smile and my mom says, "And *you* are kind-hearted. Which is why you need to talk to Kelly."

There it is. I was hoping this wouldn't come up but that's not possible since I told them everything just now. "Yeah. I know. I'll talk to her."

"Here, have this and chill," my dad says, handing me the ice cream bucket.

"Hey, how about we all watch a movie tonight?" My mom asks.

"Sounds great. Let me go change into my sweats," my dad says, heading to his room.

I was just going to tell them I didn't want to eat this ice cream alone, but my mom read my mind. Just like she always does.

We spent time watching movies, gossiping, and eating ice cream with just one spoon, and finally, decided to call it a night.

I went back to my room and checked my phone. There were four missed calls and nine texts from Kelly. I opened the texts.

Kelly: Hey! Where'd you go?

Kelly: Why aren't you answering your phone? Is everything okay?

Kelly: Okay am freaking out now.

Kelly: Are you home? Shall I come by?

Kelly: LILY!!!!!! Seriously?

Kelly: Answer your phone!

Kelly: Are you okay? Please call me.

Kelly: Did I do something? Are you mad at me?

Kelly: If so, am sorry, L! Please talk to me... :(

Wow. She must be furious *and* upset right now. I should at least text her.

Me: Hey, K! Am sorry. I felt a little dizzy, so I just had to rush back home without telling you. And I nodded off, so couldn't answer the phone. Sorry about that. Am fine now. Will talk to you tomorrow. Night! XO.

I have all the time in the world to talk about the actual issue. I don't have to rush. Or maybe I could just forget it. Now that they are together, there is no point in bringing it up. I would just be getting in their way and making unnecessary trouble. It's better if I let it go and make peace with the fact that he is dating my best friend. I must move on. Period.

My phone chimes and I see her name pop up.

Kelly: Thank God! I was really freaked out. You just woke me up with your text, by the way. But it was worth it. Sleep tight, L. See you tomorrow. XOXO.

Yeah. There is no way she would have done it if she had known.

She is my sister.

5
Sarah

Way back then...

I got my very first and only friend when I was ten years old. She was my friend from school. Her name was Ivy Mathews. She stood up for me when a bunch of bullies was bothering me and that's how we got closer. She was bolder and smarter than me in so many ways. But when it came to me, she was always sweet and loyal. I loved her the moment we were acquainted. Eventually, we became inseparable. She was all that I got. I shared everything with her. Although I was just ten, I had nothing but family stuff to share. About how I was always treated differently according to their moods, and how I had no personal space or importance. She used to cheer me up with chocolates and toys since she came from a rich family. I did experience that for a while, so I knew how it was. But she had no ill attitude. Nor was she conceited. She was the perfect friend one could ask for. We got along so well for over a year or so.

"Hey, Sarah!" She called out my name and ran towards me. She had something in her hand. Something like a box. When she reached me, she paused to take breaths and then said, "I got you a present!" She was so excited the whole time. She handed me the box. I was excited as well and opened the box with anticipation. But it was something beyond my expectations. It was a very beautiful lilac-coloured crepe swing dress. The exact one she was wearing except it was in peach.

"I thought we could wear the same kind of outfit for Christmas Eve! Isn't it great?" She asked with excitement. I couldn't react sooner. I haven't had such a beautiful dress for myself. My parents never bought me one. So, it was such a big deal for me. And the fact that it was a matching outfit made it even more special. Like we were sisters. And out of nowhere, I teared up when I said, "I love it, Ivy! Thank you so much for this." And then I hugged her. She hugged me back. It was a great moment. Again, one of the best moments I remember aside from all the worse memories that were dominating.

Ivy was my one and only hope, to survive the shit I was going through.

~~~

The other day, I went to the local market with my mother to buy groceries and I was carrying a bag of vegetables and bread. Something caught my eye and I stopped to admire it because I knew I could never buy it. I can't even remember what it was that caught my attention. The incident that happened after that was the dominating memory. After staring enough, I looked ahead to find my mother, but she was nowhere to be seen. She had left. I rushed through the crowd looking for her and yelling, "Mom!" all the way. At one point I started asking people if they had seen my mother, describing her features. Nobody seemed to have seen her. And then, the thought hit me.

Maybe she wanted me gone. That's why she left me. It wasn't like I knew the exact way to go back home. Even if I did, I have no money for the bus or a cab. I could walk...

My fearful thoughts were interrupted by a hand yanking my arm and spinning me, which made the bag fall out of my hand. And then I got this sharp pain across my cheek which brought back all the tears I was saving for later. Everyone's attention was on us. On *me*. As if slapping me on the street, in front of strangers wasn't satisfying enough for her, she yelled at me with all her energy, from the top of her lungs. I could feel the vehicles across the street halt, to see me getting yelled at. It was so humiliating and hurtful. And the fact that I couldn't say or do anything was worse than any other feeling. With everything shattering my heart, her words left me completely broken into pieces. Her exact words were, "What? Were you planning to run off with all these groceries? You are so vexatious!" I wasn't even sure what that word meant but I knew it was definitely not good.

And then she grabbed all the groceries off the ground and asked me to follow her. At that moment, I wanted to run away. So far from her, from every eye that was staring at me, and from myself for letting me get so hurt for no reason.

But all I could do was follow her, with all eyes on me, the entire way off the street. I cried the entire way home. Of course, what else could happen after such an unforgettable incident. I went to my room, locked the door, and started writing. I began writing letters to ease the pain, but it didn't really work at first. I did it anyway. That was my way of outlet for emotions. It was Ivy's advice though. She was the one who suggested I write, whenever I felt down or happy. She was almost never wrong, and I liked her a lot so I thought I could give it a try. And it grew on me. I started writing often. Things I could never tell anyone. Not even Ivy.

It did help a bit though. Not much but it was something. She also suggested that I tear it up or burn it after I was done writing. She said it might burn away my frustrating thoughts along with the paper and make me feel better. I tried once, but it didn't really have much effect. So, I thought, why waste ink, paper, and my words if it wasn't worth it? And that's how I ended up writing and saving it for God knows what.

To think about it, Ivy was almost in all my moments. Whether I shared everything with her or not, she was somehow involved in everything I did. And that made me move on. Knowing she was there for me, gave me hope and strength to endure and survive.

I was lucky enough to find her at a very young age yet at the absolute right time of my life.

~~~

I never showed the dress to my parents. I knew they wouldn't feel happy about it. So, I wore a dress that my mother had picked for me. It wasn't a new dress. It was the same dress I wore last Christmas Eve. It was a little tight, but I managed. We didn't have a tree or a cake. It was just another day. And I really didn't bother. The festive and the special occasions, everything just seemed like an excuse to have a great time with family. But when your family was a complete shit show every single day, no number of festivals or special occasions was going to change that whatsoever.

We were having dinner together though. Just as we finished, my mother handed something to my father which made him jump with joy. He then hugged my mother which was a shock to me since all he did was beat her up and yell at her.

But I thought, maybe because it was Christmas, they were acting this way. But that wasn't it. They both looked at me and my mom said, "You are going to be a sister!" And then my father kissed my mother on her forehead. I was still processing the information. Deep down I was happy about being a sister. Really excited. But the thought of that baby being born and raised in this family scared me. I had mixed emotions all over the place. But then I was met with something unexpected. Both hugged me at the same time and said, "Merry Christmas, Sarah." That lasted for at least a few seconds before they pulled away from me. Again, I was in shock and mixed with various emotions. They hadn't hugged me in a very long time. They didn't even smile at me for a long time. But that day, I got the best hug from both of them at the same time and it was good.

Maybe this baby will bring happiness back into our lives and everything could go back to normal. I wished.

Little did I know what the future had in store for me.

6

Jamie

Back then...

"Hey, we should head back now," William said, heading towards the hallway. I followed him, carrying my guitar case. I didn't think we would ace it with much less practice, but I was confident enough to think about performing solo now. At least, that's what everyone tried to tell me. And William had been pushing me to do a solo for a long time. That was a perk of knowing how to play the guitar *and* sing. People start supporting you and cheering for you, which gives a little motivation. I would like to think it's my one and only charm and talent. So, I didn't want it to go to waste. Or worse, I didn't want to screw it up. As much as I wanted to perform solo, I was also equally scared of ruining it. That was my only thing. I couldn't take risks. Not just yet. I thought I might still need some practice and self-confidence. Maybe then, I could think about it. Until then, I felt sticking to a group seemed like the best option. Also, because I was the lead vocalist.

I walked through the back entrance of the building since I had parked my car there. Or at least that's what I told myself was the reason. The actual reason I parked my car there and used the back entrance was so that I could run into her. Hoping that I would run into her. I just got addicted to her. I needed to see her at least once a day. Don't ask me why. I just did. And I hoped that one day, I would walk up to her and introduce myself.

I got out of the hallway and reached the lawn before the parking lot. I debated with myself whether to look at the bench she usually occupied or not. Because if she was not there, I might have regretted hoping for her presence. I took a whole minute to come to a decision and finally looked at the bench. And that's when I knew. There was no way I would regret anything when it came to her. A smile appeared across my face without my realization. I tried to hide it but couldn't help it. The fact that she was right there, made me happier than the applause I received for the performance.

Wait. Maybe she saw my performance. I thought.

She was alone again and had no coffee this time. She was not writing either. She was just sitting there, all beautiful, staring at the people on the lawn. Or probably just staring at the sky. Or maybe she was in a deep thought...

"Hey! Are you coming?" William interrupted my thoughts and called from a few feet away.

"I'll be there in a few," I said and turned to look at her. And the smile on my face turned into a frown.

'No, she can't. Why is she crying? Did someone hurt her? Is she in pain? I can't tell because I DON'T KNOW!'

God! I hated that I couldn't comfort her. She started walking. I hid behind the bushes and waited for her to reach a certain distance. Once she was at least ten feet away from me, I started to follow her. She passed the parking lot, which meant she didn't bring her car. She was walking.

'Great. I can observe carefully.'

But I remembered I had a guitar on my back. It was huge and noticeable. So, I went to my car and left my guitar there. I grabbed my hoodie jacket and locked the car. She almost reached the gate by then. So, I paced up a little so that I was not too far away from her. She walked as if there was no one around her. Like she was invisible. A woman bumped into her, but she didn't care. She kept walking. I knew she was not in the right place then. She must have been through something terrible. She ceased at the bus stop and took the empty seat next to an old woman. I watched her until the old woman got on the bus and left. Now, she was the only one left. Again, staring at the vehicles passing by. A bus came to a stop, but she didn't get on it. Maybe it was not the bus she was waiting for. A few more minutes passed by. Another bus came and she didn't get on it either. Maybe she was not there for the bus. Maybe she just wanted to sit there for a while and leave. I kept watching her from a few feet away and she was still as a rock. She was not crying though.

She just teared up back in college but now she was just lost. Completely lost. Heartbroken. Or in grief. No clue, but she was deeply troubled. I hated that she was going through whatever it was, all by herself.

I must do something...

I *wanted* to do something to make her feel better. I looked around and found a floral shop. I knew it was cliché, but I did it anyway. I ran to the shop and bought a bouquet of beautiful lilies. I also bought a card and placed it on the lilies. Hopefully, the flowers and the message would make her feel a glimmer of happiness. I wanted to give it to her, but I didn't want her to know it was me. I didn't want to meet her like that. Not yet. I wanted to meet her officially when she was ready and in a better mood. So, I pretended like I was talking to someone over the phone and reached the bus stand. She was seated on the rightmost seat. So, I took the one on the left. There was an empty seat between us, and I placed the flowers there. She didn't notice. I kept fake talking over the phone so that she didn't feel suspicious. But I did glance at her a time or two and that's when I realized how wrong I was about her. She was not only the most beautiful person, but she was also exceptional. I haven't even spoken a word to her, but I already admired her.

Something about her was so mesmerizing. I looked away immediately when I realized I was staring at her. I got up and started walking away. I stopped a few feet away and looked at her. She still hadn't moved. I waited for her to look to her left and then she did. It was a small turn but enough to catch her attention. Her eyes finally fell on the lilies. She stared at it for a while. And then looked up and around. Probably wondered who left it there. She then picked it up with a little hesitation, by looking around again. She handled the flowers with such care and then she looked closely for a while.

And there it was. The thing I was waiting for so badly.

Finally!

A huge smile popped across my face when I saw her smile. It was everything. I knew once again that I would do absolutely anything to see her smile. I felt light when I saw her smile. I had no idea why. It was the first time for me to act that way. But I didn't care. I liked this version of myself. And she brought out this version of me. And we hadn't even met yet. *Wow.*

I saw her wipe her cheek.

Is she crying again?

But I saw that her smile was still intact. So, it was probably a happy tear.

She finally took the bus and to my surprise, she took the flowers with her. She sat on a window seat, and I could see her happy face. I couldn't believe that it worked. It was just flowers. And she didn't get it from anyone in particular, or from anyone she knew, but she smiled and took it anyway. It was probably the message. But again, it wasn't something to get this happy and emotional.

If a tiny thing like this can make her smile, what if I could give her everything she wants?

I wanted to make sure she got everything she ever wanted.

7
Lily

Present day

I am in my class, and I don't see Kelly anywhere. I hear the bell ring and I take my phone and text her. Just as I finish my text, I see Mr. Hudson entering the class and Kelly comes in after him. I stare at her with confusion, but she looks at me with excitement. She takes the empty seat behind me, and I turn to ask her what the excitement was all about. She nudges me to look forward and just as I turn back, Mr. Hudson starts talking. "Attention, please?" He pauses and looks at everyone before talking. "It seems you will have an excursion by the end of this month. People who are in shall give their names by the end of next week."

"Uh, Mr. Hudson? Where is the trip to?" A guy asks him.

"Well, there is no final decision yet. They are still discussing, I guess. They will let you know later." Everyone starts talking and making noises. I turn to Kelly and ask, "Did you know about this?"

"Kind of. I heard one of the teachers talking to the principal."

"What were you doing in the principal's office?" I ask. She gives me a look that says I should know why. And then I remember that her mother is the receptionist in our school and her desk is near the principal's office.

"Got it. Sorry."

"Okay. Can we please get back to our class now?" Mr. Hudson says. And we all go silent and stare at him. That's how we answer him. He then starts the class.

~~~

During lunch, I get a text from someone.

Uncle Simon: How's my little girl doing? I was in your neighbourhood. Thought I would stop by.

Me: I am in school right now. Will meet you in the evening. And by the way, am not a little girl!

Uncle Simon: You are to me. :) See you in the evening.

I smile at that. I have always liked my uncle a lot. He has been such a great help to our family. Apparently, since I was a child. I heard stories about him from mom. That's how I started to like him. And when I spent enough time with him, we got really close and are basically like best friends. I think I may have many best friends, most of whom are my own family.

I wince when I hear his voice. "Hey. There you are," he says, sliding onto the bench next to Kelly. I had to scoot over to give him some room. Now they are close enough to have their own romance session. God, I feel pathetic. I know I decided to let it go and move on, but they make it so hard. Maybe I should talk to Kelly after all. But right now, I can't do this. So, I take my food tray and leave. I do tell Kelly to meet me in the class before leaving. But before I go, I look in their direction and I flinch. Because he is staring at me. For longer than two seconds this time. I look away and walk away as fast as I can. This can't be happening.

Am I going crazy, or did that really happen just now? It did look like he was staring at me. No. It's not it. Stop imagining things! He is—

I am snapped out of my thoughts when I bump into someone. A guy. The books he was holding fall to the floor and he bends over to pick those up. I help him and say, "I am sorry. I didn't see you there."

"It's okay, Lily," he says. That's when I look at him. He smiles at me. I couldn't recognize him at first but maybe that's because he used to wear glasses and have much less hair. Now he is different. He has no glasses and has messy, wavy hair with a few strands on his forehead. This look of his is so much better but makes him look less of a nerd, which he is, since he tops almost all the classes. I get up and hand him his books. He takes them from me and smiles again.

"Are you okay?" He asks.

"Oh, I am fine. Sorry again, Liam."

"Don't worry about it. I didn't see you either so, it's kind of my fault too," he says. I smile. "Uh, I should go. See you," he says and walks past me. I look over my shoulder at him and he looks at me too. But then I am interrupted by Kelly as she runs toward me. And when she reaches me, she looks at me, then at Liam, and then at me again. She gives me a crooked smile and says, "So, Liam huh?"

I look at her, flustered. And finally say, "Yeah, that was Liam." She gives me a sarcastic look. I change the subject and ask her, "What happened at lunch? You are back early."

"Oh, Gavin had practice and you left me there alone."

"Come on, I didn't leave you alone. You were with *Gavin*," I say his name with some force and walk away. She then follows me and finally starts telling me about them.

"You are probably wondering about me and Gavin."

"Not really," I sneer. She then sighs.

"Come on, Lil."

"Fine. Since you brought it up, I must ask this. How the hell did you end up with him? And *when*?" She smiles in return.

"Oh, my god. Are you blushing?" I scoff.

"It was yesterday. At my party." I look at her in shock.

Yesterday? That soon? She never said she liked him in the first place. Well, I didn't tell her either so it's not my place to judge or feel this way.

"I know what you are thinking. I should have told you sooner about how I felt about him."

"Hey, no it's okay. I mean it is sudden, of course, but I am happy for you. Really." *I am happy for her.*

"I knew you would understand," she says and hugs me sideways. I chose not to tell her about my feelings. I mean, it won't matter now, so why bother? Besides, I didn't *like* him, like him. It was just a crush. It will go away. Eventually. Hopefully.

~~~

I reach home and Uncle Simon is already there. A huge smile appears on my face and on his face as well. We hug each other and he playfully tousles my hair as we sit on the couch. "So, what's new?" I ask him. He turns to face me with his left hand propping his head, on the couch. "Well, I am getting married. That's what's new," he says with a straight face. I, on the other hand, am stoked.

"Really? To Lydia?" I ask, unable to hide the excitement.

"No, no. To wonder woman," he says in a sarcastic tone. He was always funny, and sarcastic and I love that about him. I just can't help it, so I hug him again and say, "Oh, my God am so happy for you guys! This is so amazing! Why didn't she come along?"

He pulls away from me and says, "She is already planning for the wedding and is quite busy discussing it with your mother." I look at him with a questionable expression and then it turns into a smile. "Wait, she is here?"

"No, no. She is in Turkey, where your mother is." He never ceases to amaze me. I nudge him playfully and head to the kitchen. And I see my mom leaning on the counter while she talks to Lydia. Not everyone has gorgeous red hair like her. I run toward them and hug Lydia from behind and say, "Oh, my God! I am so happy you guys are getting married." I am still hugging her when she says, "Me too, sweetie. I wanted to tell you the news, by the way. Your Uncle beat me to it."

I pull away from her and hold her hands. And then I notice her ring. "Holy moly! That's a huge ring."

"I know. *Doctor* Simon Richard, thank you very much," she says, winking at me.

"I still can't believe you said yes to my brother, of all the people," my mother says with a scoff.

"Yeah, I ask myself why sometimes but then remember that he is the sweetest guy I have ever met. Also, his sense of humour."

"Yeah, sweet, and funny. That's a rare combination," I say in agreement. "But he is also super smart. And not to mention, handsome."

She blushes and nods. "Anyway, where is Jamie?" She asks. And then I go, "Oh, you don't know? He owns an instrument store."

"Musical instruments? So do you have like, all kinds of instruments?"

"Yep. And he also takes classes. Guitar and vocals," I say with content.

"Wow. That is so cool," she says.

"It is. It's always been his dream," my mother says, with a proud look on her face.

"Wait. Does dad not know about you guys yet?"

"No, honey. I was just about to call him though."

"Don't! I am going to meet him at the store. I'll take Uncle Simon with me." My mom and Lydia glance at each other and then she says, "Okay. Then I and your *Aunt* Lydia will make dinner." At that, I smile at Lydia, and she hugs me saying, "You are the sweetest niece one could ask for." To that, I say, "Well, then you are lucky you are marrying my uncle."

~~~

We meet my father at his store, and he looks happy when he sees us walking in. "Hey!" He says with his hands up in the air. But before we could go to him, a customer comes to the counter with a guitar. My father attends to him and waves his hand, gesturing for us to sit on the couch, by the window. Before I could reach the couch, the customer with the guitar turns, and to my surprise, its Liam.

"Hey, Lily," he greets me with a smile and with a hint of astonishment in his expression.

"Hey, Liam," I say and look at the guitar. "Good choice."

He looks at the guitar and then says, "Oh, thank you. I just completed my lessons for good. I think I can play with confidence now."

"Wow. That's great"!

I had no idea he had interests other than academics. But it's cool.

"Yeah, well, Mr. Brooks was a great coach," he says, pointing his thumb over his shoulder, at my dad. I look over his shoulder at my dad and say, "Yeah. He is the best."

"Oh, are you learning an instrument as well?" He asks with curiosity. I shake my head and say, "No, he is my dad." He doesn't speak for a few seconds and gives me a look that says, '*No Way!*' But then his expression changes. Like everything adds up and finally makes sense.

"Lily *Brooks*," he finally says. I nod with a tight-lipped smile.

"Wow. That is so awesome. Jamie Brooks, the cool musician, is your father! I mean, his songs are one of a kind. He has a great voice and the way he plays the guitar, my God!" He sounds excited.

"Yeah!" I say with the same amount of excitement. I really enjoy it when other people look up to my dad and are his fans. "I am glad you got to be his student."

"Are you kidding? This was a memorable experience for me. I am not just glad; I am super blessed to have met your father. And the fact that he was my coach is way more than a blessing."

Wow.

"I didn't know you liked music. I always thought of you as the geek who doesn't really have other interests." The moment I say those words, I regret it. He looks at me with a dissatisfied look and I feel terrible.

"God, I am sorry, Liam. I didn't mean it that way. I just always saw you with your books and you are a straight-A student so—", he snaps at me and says, "Nah, it's fine. I always get that. Actually, you are the only one so far to know this about me," he points at his guitar. And then I ask him something I never expected I would ask.

"If you don't mind, can you tutor me?" He looks at me all confused. "Math. I am weak at math. That's what I need tutoring with." He smiles and relief washes over me. "Sure. I will let you know the deets later," he says and heads toward the door. I turn and say, "Thank you!"

He turns and nods with a smile. When I walk toward the couch, both my dad and uncle Simon are having coffee and reminiscing about the time when my dad and mum got married, about how they were excited to have me, and how close I and Uncle Simon got. I stood there for a while listening to them talk and it was so refreshing. When my dad finally noticed me, he calls me to the couch, and I take a seat between them.

"You know that kid?" My dad asks. I nod. "He is in my class. Oh, and he is your fan."

"Yeah, he might have mentioned something about it to me when I was coaching him," he says, with a delighted look on his face. I look at him and he gives me a comical smile.

"I asked him if he would help me with math."

"Oh, that's good. What did he say?"

"He said he would tutor me."

"You guys are so cute," Uncle Simon admits. My dad nods in agreement. I can't help but laugh.

"Uh, he is a brilliant student. That's why I asked him. Besides, we just met."

"You just said he was in your class," my uncle points out. And then they both laugh. I shake my head and change the subject. I turn to Uncle Simon and ask, "When is the big day?"

"Well, Lydia wants a June wedding."

"That's just a few months away," I say. But then I remembered something. I turn to my dad and say, "You and mom got married in June!"

"What? Really? Was it June?" He asks sardonically. Sometimes I wonder if my dad and Uncle Simon are related since they both are alike. "Uh-huh!" I say, making a silly face and then I turn to face my uncle again.

"What if you guys got married on the same day as my parents' wedding anniversary? It would be two celebrations at once. It would be amazing. What say?" I can no longer hide my enthusiasm as I wait for him to answer. When he finally answers, I jump up with joy and clap my hands like a kid who just got candies and toys.

"Well, this is going to be a memorable wedding," my dad says looking at my uncle. And he responds with, "Yeah, tell me about it," with his brows arched and a grin.

8
Sarah

Way back then...

On my twelfth birthday, my parents decided to tell me I was adopted. No, my *adoptive* parents decided to tell me I was adopted. I think it's the best gift parents could ever give a child on his or her birthday. However, it didn't really affect me since I kind of already knew I was adopted. I had doubts when my classmates pointed out the fact about how different I looked from others. I realized how different I looked from my parents. My father was a brunette, and my mother was a blonde. I thought I got my hair from my dad but then the looks and skin tone didn't make sense. According to Ivy, I looked half Asian. She knew her stuff.

And to top all that, the way they treated me proved my doubts. No parent would treat their children like trash. Or at least that's what I thought. I was sure I was adopted when I was ten but never really confronted them. I don't know why. Maybe I was grateful that they adopted me when my birth parents thought I was not worth raising. That is the only reason I had to bear with them, no matter how harsh they were towards me.

When they broke the news to me, I didn't really give them the response that they might have expected and went back to my room. Because I didn't want to give them the satisfaction of feeling the aftermath of telling a kid that she was adopted on her *birthday*. How merciless and stone-hearted they had to be to tell something like that to a girl on her birthday. But little did they know that I was already broken inside. At the age of twelve, at that. I was already done with birthdays, so I didn't expect anything special, but what they did was a surprise. I wasn't surprised that I was adopted since I already knew it. I was surprised by the fact that they chose to tell me that on my birthday. But the best part was that I didn't cry that day. It was the first birthday in a long time that I didn't cry. I wrote though, having no one to share my sorrows and shit with. That's how I spent the whole day. In my room, writing and sleeping. But not even a single tear was shed. I was proud. *Maybe I am finally growing up*, I thought.

Aside from all the bad days, the one thing that made me go on, was the fact I was going to be a sister. I still remember how they reacted when they found out she was pregnant. They were sweet to me too. But that was it. Ever since that day, there were no happy moments with them. I figured maybe the news was the only reason for their happy mood and not the fact that they enjoyed sharing the news with me.

It made sense though. They adopted me since they couldn't conceive. But later, when they did, they were filled with nothing but joy. So, they reacted the way they did and treated me like their own for once. But I didn't care about any of those, as long as I could be a part of it. All I cared about was the baby and how I was going to be his/her sister, that is if they allowed it. I was always scared they wouldn't let me meet the baby and get to know him or her. I hoped I could be a part of that baby's life since I thought only the baby's presence could make me feel better.

~~~

I was laying on my bed and staring at the ceiling when there was a knock on the door. I opened the door and saw a couple standing.

They had no faces. Or they were masked. I couldn't tell. I stared at them long enough and finally asked, "Who are you?"

They kept standing still and after a few seconds, the lady took a step forward. I took a step backward. Then she stopped. The man was still standing in the doorway. The lady finally took another step toward me and this time, I didn't move. She kneeled before me and said, "I am sorry, dear." I looked at her with confusion. And then the man said, "We didn't think you would suffer this much." He kneeled beside the lady and they both were looking at me. The weird part was that I could see their eyes but not their faces. I could see the tears flowing but not their expressions since I couldn't see their entire faces. "Can I see your faces?" I asked. They looked at each other and then at me. After a while, they stood up and took a step back. I was still staring at them, all flustered and in disbelief. I got this sudden chill and realization of who they might be. They were still standing a foot away from me, not responding.

I took in a sharp breath and said the words, "Are you, my birth parents?" They still stood unresponsive and looked at each other again. A few seconds passed, and they both move their hands to their respective faces, probably in an attempt to remove their masks or to show me their faces or to God knows what.

I was still waiting for them to do it, but I got the urge to close my eyes. So, I squeezed my eyes shut and waited.

"Just know that we love you, sweetheart," I heard the man say. "And we are truly sorry," they both said in unison. Just as I heard their voices, I forced open my eyes, just to end up staring at the ceiling again.

The tears I thought were long gone flowed like a river when I realized it was just a dream.

To me though, it was a *nightmare.*

9

Jamie

·◦·♡·◦·

Back then...

My father was an alcoholic, a gambler, and the worst example of how a father should be. Ever since I was a kid, he has never been a good father. No, let me rephrase that. He has never been a *father* to me. From a very young age, since my mother died of cancer, I had to do all the chores, had to pay for my own classes and I had to take care of my father. He was fine until my mother passed away. He couldn't digest the fact that she left him and started drinking like it was the only solution to his problem. He didn't care about the only son he had. Whatever little money I saved up, he used it for booze and gambling. He was such an ass. I knew the death of my mom affected him but that doesn't justify his actions towards his son who was also grieving his mother's death and had to do a lot on his own. I hated him. Hatred is barely a word when I think about what I went through with him. I loathed him, from the bottom of my heart. Yet, I found myself in front of his grave every year since he died of alcohol poison. I didn't intend to visit him, but I ended up there anyway. I guess a parent's death does that to you. You feel obligated to do all of this even if you don't feel like it from your heart. At least, not to a parent like him. My mother, on the other hand, was great. Although, I didn't have many good memories with her. All the memories I had of her, were from when she was under chemo. But I still enjoyed every day with her. She did everything she could for me till the day she was alive. Unlike my father. My father was probably a good husband to my mother since she was never unhappy with him. I guess I could give him that. But other than that, he was a complete nuisance.

On my way back, I stopped at a café to ease myself. Nothing a cup of coffee couldn't fix. I walked in and there were a couple of people waiting to order. As I waited in line, I thought of what to order. When I finally decided what I wanted, I was at the counter and a woman was clearing up the bill, with her head down. I waited for her to ask for my order and when she lifted her head, my mind went blank. My mouth seemed to have forgotten how to open up to speak and had lost the capacity to make up the words.

"What would you like to have, sir?" I thought that was what she asked because I didn't hear anything at that moment. All I saw was her in front of me, on that day.

'What are the chances?'

"Excuse me, Sir? Are you alright?" She waved her hand in front of my eyes and it snapped me out of whatever it was. I could finally make up words and my mouth could finally speak. "Uh, can I get an iced white chocolate mocha, please?"

"Sure sir," she said and smiled. *God, that smile.*

"Your good name sir?" She asked.

"Jamie. Jamie Brooks," I said. She nodded with a smile. I wanted to know her name. So, I looked at her name tag and it said, "Sarah."

'Sarah. That's a pretty name. But she is much prettier.'

"That will be $3.8, Mr. Brooks." I paid her and asked her the one thing that has been nagging me since I saw her there. "Do you recognize me?" She looked at me for a moment and went, "I think I do." My level of happiness rose to ecstatic when she said that. I couldn't help but smile. She smiled too. And she said, "Here is your iced white chocolate mocha, Mr. Brooks," handing me the cup.

I took it from her and replied with, "Thank you, Sarah." I could see her eyes flicker but then she smiled and that was the best thing that happened to me that day.

I took a seat by the window which seemed to be isolated like no one ever sat there. But I liked that seat since I had the perfect view of her. And she could see me too. But she hadn't looked at me once since I sat there. I was almost done with my coffee, but she seemed busy.

'Damn these customers. How come she is the only one? Why aren't there any shifts? She must be tired of doing it all by herself.'

I couldn't leave without talking to her now. She said she recognized me. I had to know. Even if I had to stay there all day. Once I was done with my coffee, I went for a refill. And when I was at the counter again, she looked at me and said, "Wow. You must have a rough day."

"You have no idea," I said in reply. When she brought me another cup, I asked her, "When does your shift end?" She looked over her shoulder at her boss and said, "At five."

I looked at my watch and the time was 3:50. I could hear her giggle when I looked at my watch. "Here. Just wait for an hour and I'll see you," she said. I paid her, grabbed the cup, and headed to the same seat. This time, I made sure I didn't drink my coffee too fast. An hour was not that bad. It was just sixty minutes. Just three thousand six hundred seconds. It was not that big a deal.

But it felt like an eternity. And after my fourth cup of coffee, she finally came up to me and said, "Hey. I am done with my shift."

"You have no idea how much I wanted to hear you say that." She laughed and nudged me towards the door.

"Okay, but before we go, can I get a cup of coffee?"

She cracked up and went, "What?"

"Yeah, I got tired of having coffee and waiting for you."

"So, you want another cup of *coffee* to make you feel better?"

"Yep," I said with a nod, and it made her laugh so hard. I loved the sound she made when she laughed. I could hear her laugh all day long.

"Okay, let me get you one," she said, but I stopped her.

"What kind of a guy would I be if I let a pretty woman like you, do errands for me?" Again, I saw her smile. Third time in a row. That was an achievement.

I got another cup of coffee to go, and we just walked in silence for a few moments. And then, I finally broke the silence with, "So, you know who I am?" She looked at me and said, "Yeah, you are Jamie Brooks," looking ahead. And now, I laughed. "Yep. The one and only," I said.

"I saw you perform once. You had this amazing energy, and your voice was so soothing." I looked at her like I couldn't take my eyes off her, because if I did, I was afraid she might disappear.

"It was peaceful to hear you sing and so cool to hear you play your guitar."

I had never been complimented like that. Or at least, I didn't remember ever getting a compliment like that. And now, I didn't care about any other compliments but that one.

"And then I saw you out on the lawn when I was waiting for my friend. I knew it was you, even though I didn't see you up close. Your hair is indelible," she said, pointing to my hair. "I waved at you and felt instant regret." At that, I gave her a questionable look. She continued. "I mean, it was like a 'ridiculous fan moment' if you will. I saw you, got star-struck, and waved at you like a crazy fan. But you stood still, and I knew I freaked you out," she said, with a laugh. "It was embarrassing. So, I left."

"Just so you know, I wasn't freaked out and I don't think it was ridiculous. I mean I was shocked to be smiled at, by a beautiful woman if *you* will." She chuckled and said, "You are just saying that, so I don't feel awkward."

"No, I am really not. I mean it." She looked at me sideways and continued. "And the third time I saw you was when you left a bouquet of lilies for me at the bus stop." I was perplexed and when I looked at her, she went, "What? You think a hoodie makes you invisible?" she sneered. And I was embarrassed.

"I knew it was you when I saw the 'J' on the message you left. I actually knew your name. I sort of wanted to ask you why you did that, but after seeing you try so hard as to not let me know it was you, I didn't ask you." She looked ahead, letting me know that she was done. So, I started talking now. "You have no clue how happy that makes me, Sarah. I have wanted to talk to you and know you so badly, that I kept thinking about you every day. And the other day, when I saw you cry, I just couldn't stay still. I had to do something, even if it was the bare minimum. And I can't believe that a bunch of lilies made you smile like that."

"For your information, lilies are my favourite. So, I was happy when I got them, along with a sweet message. And the fact that it was from you, made my day. That is why I smiled."

'Wow. Lilies are her favourite. What are the chances? I know her already. We are made for each other.'

We just exchanged gaze at each other for a while and then she said, "I know what you are thinking."

'That I might be falling for you.'

"Uh, what?"

"You are thinking, so much has happened between us already and you still don't know my last name, right?"

'That was so not what I was thinking, but I would like to know your last name as well.'

Before I could ask, she said, "Richard. I am Sarah Richard. But I would rather you call me Sarah. So...it's nice to finally meet you, J," she said, extending her hand. I shook her hand and said, "Pleasure to meet you, Miss Sarah."

We smiled at each other while my mind did its own thinking.

'Sarah Brooks. Sounds perfect!'

10

Lily

Present day

"How come we never thought of this?" Lydia asks Uncle Simon, placing her hands on his shoulder. I watch them as I get myself a drink from the kitchen and they look so adorable. "Because sweetie, we are dumb," he responds with a nod and that made her laugh. He then moves a strand of her hair from her face. I go to my room and sit at my desk. I can still hear them giggle all the way in here. *They are loud as children, I gotta say.*

I like how they make each other feel. It's so cute and *romantic*. Speaking of romantic, my parents top the list. My dad has told me a lot of stories from when they were dating, and it was so sweet and perfect just to hear them. My mother was the one who suggested I hear it from my father since he can tell a story in an engaging way. He told me every little detail of how they met, how they got close, and how they ended up getting married. It was so beautiful; I was envious of them. I want what they had. What they *have*. I have never seen them argue or fight. Almost all married couples have fights and misunderstandings from time to time, but my parents never had one. Or maybe they did a great job hiding it from me. Either way, it's so cool that sometimes, I doubt if they are even real. Because from what I heard, and from the looks of their relationship, it seems so unrealistic. Like a fairy tale, where everything is beautiful with unrealistic scenarios and happy endings. That never happens in real life but with my parents, it seems like their own fairy tale where they got their happy ending and are still living it, *happily*. That is just a dream for most people, including me. I mean, things like this can happen, sure. But it's rare. *Unique*. Just because it happened with my parents doesn't mean it can happen to me. Or it *might*. Now that I look at what Uncle Simon and Aunt Lydia have, there is a possibility that I can get that too. I like to believe that someday, I get to have my own fairy tale with someone special.

"Hey! There's my girl," someone calls out and hugs me from behind. I turn just enough to look at her face and I jump with joy and give her a perfect hug. "Hey, Aunt Ivy! It's been so long. How are you?"

Did I mention that she is like the best Aunt in the whole world? Well, she *is* the best Aunt in the whole world. Even if she is not related to me. But now, maybe she has a competitor.

"I am fine darling. I came in and saw Simon and his fiancé. I didn't see your parents though. Simon told me you were in your room and the door was ajar so I just sneaked in. So, how is my beautiful niece?" She asks, stroking my hair.

"Well, as you can see, I am *Bitchin'*."

"Atta girl!" She says, with a wink.

"By the way, what's with the sudden visit?" I ask.

"Well, I missed you guys so much, and I am only free for a few days. Also, your birthday is in a few days so I thought I would spend some time with you until your birthday."

Wow. I forgot about my birthday being so close.

The look on my face makes Aunt Ivy ask the thing she is about to ask. "Lily Brooks? Did you forget about your birthday?"

I don't answer but give her a slow nod.

"How held up are you, that you don't remember your birthday nearing? You must be really busy."

"Not really. It's just that, I...I don't know."

"Wow. Your life must be miserable." I laugh because it's the exact opposite. "Aunt Ivy? I think it's completely normal for these things to happen. Besides, I didn't forget my birthday *on* my birthday," I point out. I don't even know why it's a big deal. But she has always been like this. She is also a drama queen. Hence, the reaction.

"Hey, Ivy?" My dad calls.

"Hey, Jamie!" She exclaims and hugs him.

"Long time. How are you?" He asks. She pulls away from him to answer him but then she sees my mother and goes, "Oh, my God! There she is," and gives her a tight hug. "Clearly, she is the same old Ivy," my dad says with a side nod.

My mother is super excited when she says, "What a pleasant surprise. I missed you."

"Aw, me too, hon," she says, and finally pulls away from her. "By the way, I saw Simon and Lydia. They just said they got engaged. This is huge!" She says with excitement.

"I know, right? There is more. They are going to get married on my parent's wedding day," I add.

"No way!" She exclaims. "That's a double celebration."

"That's what I said!" I exclaim and then we high-five and hug it out.

"Okay. Again, you two are the exact same person in two different bodies. We get it," my dad mocks us, and Aunt Ivy elbows him by the side. "Where is William by the way?" My dad asks.

"Oh, he had an important business meeting, so he couldn't make it. But he did say he would be here a day before Lily's birthday," she says winking at me. Uncle William, my *dad's* friend who got married to my *mom's* friend is also an interesting human. But unlike Uncle Simon or my dad, he is not a fan of jokes or humour in general. Although he enjoys sarcasm occasionally, he hates it when someone does it to him. But he is a sweet person. Sort of.

"The man's always busy, ain't he?"

"What do I say? It's as if he is the only one running the company. Never has much free time. Always gets home exhausted. I feel terrible for him." She sounds doubtful. As if she doesn't believe her own words that came out of her mouth. Before I could ask, my mom beats me to it.

"Ivy? Is everything okay with you two? I mean, do think he is—"

"No! hey, come on," she cuts her off. "No. It's just...I don't know. Forget it. Let's focus on the big picture here," she says with a fake smile. She is such a see-through person.

"Guys! Let's have a party tonight," Lydia yells as she makes her way to my room but stops when she senses the tension between us.

"Is...everything okay over here?" She asks as she looks from my dad to Aunt Ivy and to my mom.

"Yeah, everything is fine. You are right, let's have a party tonight. What say, guys?" I ask, breaking the silence and looking at everyone. Finally, my mom says, "Yeah. Let's have a party. Come on, guys. Let's prepare for the party," she says, going back into the house.

"Honey? Call Kelly and some other friends of yours."

"On it!"

11

Sarah

---♡---

Way back then...

I remember the very first time I held Simon. It was a few days after his birth, and he was this cute, little chubby human who was unbelievably perfect. I could feel that he was already adapting to me. He looked safe and happy when he was with me. I was surprised that Mrs. Richard was fine with me getting along with her son. Ever since they broke the news about me being adopted, I stopped addressing them as mom and dad. I didn't even call them mom and dad after that, and they seemed fine with it.

Of course. What else is new?

But I realized the reason for them being okay with me spending time with Simon was that they needed a rest. And I was their maid/babysitter who didn't charge them for my time and work. Although I was fine with it, I still cried myself to sleep. It took me less than thirty seconds to cry for all kinds of silly reasons. If someone wanted me to cry, all they had to do was to ask me how I was doing. And the tears would flow like a river. I didn't know how and when it got that worse. I just knew I cried every day since the day I was treated like a piece of crap. I got used to it, but it still hurt and every little act of theirs made me shed tears.

But I didn't mind and tolerated it, as long as I could be with Simon. Taking care of him and playing with him was the best diversion for me but most importantly, I loved him so much. But ever since he was born, the little attention I used to get, was completely ceased. I wouldn't call it attention. It was their way of making sure I was still with them to do their work all the while hurting and torturing me.

I was kicked out of my own room since the baby needed one. I had to sleep on the couch in the living room. It was cold but bearable. I tried not to let it bother me since it was for the baby, but it still hurt. I always tried to forget and avoid these feelings, but it was just too difficult. I was no longer a member of that family because that is how they treated me and behaved. The feeling was mutual though. I didn't consider them as my family any more than they did. But I loved Simon. He was my brother. Even though we weren't related, he was my only family, and I would do anything to protect him and make him happy. I have always wanted a younger sibling and he was the best baby brother one could ask for. Besides, he was the only human to not treat me like a worthless crap. At least, not yet. I would've been astonished if they ever cared about me again. Which was highly unlikely.

~~~

The other day, I had to rush back home from school since I had severe pain in my stomach only to find out that I got my period. I saw Mrs. Richard on the couch with Simon on her lap and I told her about it. And all she could say was, "There are tampons on my nightstand drawer. Use them."

Of course, she had the baby to care for, but she could not care less about a teenager hitting puberty, which happens only once in a lifetime. Still, I didn't mind. Her actions stopped bothering me for good, but they did anger me. I had to learn how to use a tampon on my own. I had to go through the pain and do the chores for her. I also had to get the groceries when all she did was sleep most of the time. It wasn't like she was focusing on the baby all the time. If she had, I wouldn't have been bothered so much. But all she did was feed him when he cried at times and put him to nap. She wouldn't even change his diapers. She would sleep even when he cried. Most of the time, I was the one to change his diapers, make the formula and feed him when he was hungry, and put him to sleep. I wondered if he was properly taken care of when I was at school. And Mr. Richard was never really at home. When he was at home, he would be drunk and useless. I can't even remember a day when he spent quality time with his toddler son. All he did was work, which was not much since it wasn't a perfect job, and drink.

He didn't earn much and most of the money he did earn was spent on alcohol. He drank his sorrows away since he didn't have a good job and was not earning enough to support his family. And now that there was a baby in the picture, the pressure just increased, and he did everything in his power to lose control by turning into an alcoholic and abusive. He hit his wife a lot since he couldn't satisfy their basic needs. And the reason was that his wife gave birth to a baby when their life was not stable enough. He blamed her for everything like it was *her* fault. She endured it. No idea why.

Maybe she did care about the baby more than I thought. But I couldn't defend her as I used to before. I did try and got blamed by her as if it was all *my* fault. That's when I realized, these people were brilliant at blaming others. It was their expertise. No matter what problem or mistake was done by them, they were always ready to put the blame on others. In this case, it was me. Actually, all of the blame was poured on me, ever since I have known them. When I didn't defend her, she would later yell at me for not helping and defending her. It was their fight and their problem. Who am I to meddle?

But after a while, they would make up and act as if nothing happened. This was a never-ending loop, and I was always the victim. All I cared about was how I could protect Simon from all of it. He was still a kid but in no time, he would grow up and realize how messed up his family was. I didn't want that for him. He deserved a peaceful, happy family.

Another incident where Simon was partly involved in the mess was when Mrs. Richard was in the kitchen and Simon was in his baby cradle, playing with his rattle toy. Mr. Richard came home, all drunk and yelling. "Margret!" He yelled and made his way to the kitchen. I was in the living room, mopping the floor. It was a usual routine for him to get home drunk and make a scene. But that day was too much. "Do you have any idea how much I suffer because of you? All you do is stay home and rest while I work my ass off to run this family," he said unsteadily. Then he grabbed her arm and slapped her. I didn't move. I couldn't. I just stood there and watched. She yanked her arm and pushed him away but that didn't help. He came back with much force and pushed her which made her fall to the floor. She cried and yelled, "You aren't the only one busting your ass off for this family. I take care of our baby all day long while you drink and ruin our lives!"

He didn't speak for a while and then turned to Simon. The look he had was furious. He reached his cradle and said, "You are the reason we are suffering; you little dumb creature." I couldn't see clearly from where I was standing but I could swear, he was trying to strangle him. Before I knew it, I was next to him, yanking him away from Simon. He cried his eyes out while I was trying to calm him down. And suddenly, I felt a tight grip on my hair. Mr. Richard grabbed my hair and slammed me against the kitchen door. I couldn't move from the pain. I tried and retaliated by forcing myself to push him and elbowed him hard on his chest. He stumbled back and Mrs. Richard stepped forward and slapped me.

"How dare you hit him? After everything he has done for you." I gave her a look of disgust and confusion.

"He just hit you and tried to strangle your son!" I yelled.

"He would never do that. He was just trying to hold him, and you intercepted."

"Oh please! That's utter bullshit," I yelled. They stared at me.

"Are you that naïve?" I asked out of frustration. "Or are you just faking it?"

She didn't respond. She helped Mr. Richard to his feet and left the room. I was left alone with Simon and all I could think of was, how I had to keep him safe from those two. I thought that the reason they treated me the way they did was that I wasn't their actual child. But now that I saw them doing it to Simon made me realize that maybe they weren't fit for parenting. The fact that they were ill-treating their own son who was just a toddler, proved me right about the thought I had about them.

They were the *best* example of the *worst* parents. Period.

They would've made the best parents if they never existed.

12
Jamie

Back then...

We had our very first kiss on her birthday which was just three days ago. I was still reliving it. I was still shaken. Because *she* was the one to initiate the kiss. Although it was one of the best things ever, I was taken aback. Also, kind of ruined my plan to give her the best first kiss she has ever experienced. But that didn't matter anymore since she admitted that it was the best kiss she ever had.

Apparently, her first kiss was the worst for her. She was forced by the guy she was dating to kiss him, even though she refused. She dumped him after that though. In my case, neither was she forced, nor did I refuse. In fact, she asked me before doing it. Her exact words were, "Can I kiss you now?"

The question was shocking because it was unexpected. But most of all, it was alluring. I didn't respond though. I couldn't get the words out of my mouth. Nor did I refuse. She took that as a hint, and I was glad she did. At first, it was just a peck. When she was slowly pulling away from me, I leaned in and kissed her. The air around us was filled with palpable tension. She welcomed me by wrapping her arms around my neck, and the kiss lasted for almost a minute. The whole time, she was just as nervous as I was. Still, it was perfect.

I was lying on my bed, reminiscing, when I got a text from her.

Sarah: Hey, J. Are you free?

'Her timing couldn't be more perfect.'

Me: Yeah, love. What is it?

Sarah: Great. Let me in.

And there was a knock on the door. I rushed to the door, with very less time to process, and then I met with a sudden, screaming little boy with a scary mask on his face. From the looks of it, he was probably trying to scare me. So, I played along.

"Oh, my God! What is this creature you have brought along with you?" I yelled and covered my face. I heard him laugh and say, "You are so good at faking it. Much better than my sister."

'Smart kid.'

"You got me there, kid."

"I am not a kid!" The kid argued, which was so adorable.

"You're right. My apologies, young man," I said, with a head bow. He smiled and replied, "You are forgiven, Jamie." That made me smile.

"Hey now. Address him with respect," Sarah said to him.

"No. I prefer Jamie," I said in return. I extended my hand to him and said, "It's a pleasure to meet you." He shook my hand and replied, "Same. You can call me Simon by the way."

'I love this kid already.'

"Simon. The name clearly suits you," I said with a wink. He winked back, or at least that's what I thought he did because it was not exactly a wink since he just blinked both of his eyes. But it was cute to see him attempt.

"Hey, sorry to bother you but could you take care of him for like an hour? I have my shift at the cafe now and Ivy is not home today," Sarah said.

"Yeah, sure. I was bored anyway. Besides, this is the first time we are meeting each other. We're going to have fun, aren't we, buddy?"

"Yeah!" He exclaimed. His excitement made me excited. I had wanted to meet Sarah's brother ever since I had known about him and now seemed like the perfect time to get acquainted. And I thought it would go well.

"Okay, well you guys have fun. And thank you for this," she said, giving me a quick peck on the cheek. "And you," she pointed at Simon and went, "Behave." He nodded and waved his hand.

She left and the next couple of hours passed by, with nothing but loads of fun.

He dozed off on my lap as we watched cartoons and every now and then, he would babble in his sleep which was so funny, that I giggled. I turned off the television and carried him to my bed. Just as I tucked him in, I heard the front door open. "Jamie?" She called out. I stepped into the living room and told her that he was asleep, with a gesture. She nodded and fell onto the couch. I sat beside her, and we just sat there, quiet for a while. I finally broke the silence and said, "Rough day?" She sighed as her head falls back on the couch. "There were a lot of customers than usual. The café was filled with people today. I can't believe people crave caffeine at night." She was staring at the ceiling and looked way prettier from this angle. She caught me staring at her and said, "You do realize you look like a creep when you do that, right?" I chuckled. And then, she did. "Thanks for today, by the way," she said.

"Anytime," I smiled and said with a side nod. "Besides, we had a lot of fun. Your brother is precious. Just like someone I know," I smirked and touched her nose with the tip of my finger. She smiled. And then, we made eye contact for a few seconds. That's when I noticed her necklace. The necklace that I had given her as a birthday present, was around her neck. It was like it was made only for her neck. It belonged there. She caught me looking at her necklace and then held it in front. It was a rose gold coloured necklace and had a pendant with glass, resin, and purple dried flowers. It reminded me of her.

Delicate and beautiful.

"This is the best piece of jewellery I have ever owned. It's so pretty I almost don't want to wear it at all. But I also can't *not* wear it when it's this pretty. And most importantly, this is a reminder of you," she said and kissed me. I leaned in and kissed her back with everything I had. It was slow and deep, but a sudden sound disrupted it.

"Sarah?" Simon called out, still half asleep and rubbing his eyes. She pulled away from me and headed toward him. He probably didn't witness it since he was still rubbing his eyes and hadn't opened them yet. She kneeled in front of him and asked if they should leave. He nodded his sleepy head. She gave me a hug and said, "Good night, J."

"Bye, Jamie," Simon managed to say. I smiled and tousled his hair. And then, I looked at her. I don't know if it was because she was leaving, but I seemed to miss her like crazy when she was right here in front of me.

"Stay the night," I said. I could see her tense up. "Simon is almost asleep anyway. And you are probably exhausted from all the work. Stay here tonight. You can use my bed. I can sleep on the couch," I clarified. "You can relax and sleep tight." Her expression turned into a grateful smile. "Thank you, babe," she said, squeezing my hand. Then she headed to my room, with sleepy Simon. A few seconds later, she came back and held me from behind. We stayed like that for a while. Then she reached my ear and whispered, "I love you." She went back into the room without waiting for my response. I literally felt like the world was beneath me. The words I had been waiting to hear were finally delivered in the most beautiful way, by the most beautiful person on the most beautiful night.

'I love you too, Sarah.

I have, ever since I laid my eyes on you for the first time.

And I always will.'

13

Lily

All I did was ask Kelly to invite a few friends over to my house. Now it is so crowded, that I can barely pass from one room to the other. There are lots of people I don't really recognize. Maybe they are Kelly's friends of friends. She does know how to party. I do see Gavin. The one person I didn't want to see. But that is not possible since he is dating my best friend.

Ugh, I hate this.

"Waiting for someone?" His voice makes me flinch and I realize that I was staring at the door. I turn and say, "No, I was just trying to get past and look for Kelly."

Liam says, "Hold on," and tries to get a bunch of people away from my way. I smile at him and walk toward the door, but I am interrupted by Aunt Ivy. She grabs my arm and says, "I got you something." I follow her to the room, and she takes out a package and hands it to me saying, "Here."

"What is it?" I ask, taking it and figuring out what it might be.

"It's your birthday present."

I look at her for a moment. "Aren't you gonna be here on my birthday? You said you came here for that."

55

She doesn't respond. I can see her trying to come up with an excuse. Maybe it has something to do with Uncle William. She was fine until we brought him up. "Aunt Ivy? Are you okay?" I ask. "You can talk to me. You know that right?"

She gives me a tight-lipped smile and hugs me. "Of course. My little girl has grown so well." She pulls away and asks me to open the package. I do.

Is that a photo album?

I open it and the first picture I see is my dad holding my mom from behind. She has a beautiful smile on her face as she looks at him. It is the best picture of my parents. There are a few more of my parents hugging and laughing. There is one photo where my mom and Aunt Ivy are on a swing. They look so young. Probably in their early twenties. And the next photo is of my dad and Uncle William on a bench eating ice cream. They look young too.

This is a memory album of my parents.

There is another picture where my mom and Aunt Ivy are wearing matching dresses. Now I know why my mom wanted me and Kelly to wear matching outfits. It's so cute and they look so pretty.

"What do you think?"

"I love it! Thanks, Aunt Ivy," I say. "Aren't mom and dad so cute as a couple?"

"They are the best couple I have ever known," she says, looking at the picture and smiling. "Not every couple is happy." When she says that, I can see her eyes flicker. She obviously doesn't want to talk about it. So, I divert it.

"You know, I have never seen my parents fight or argue," I say, as a matter of fact. "I mean, there is no way a couple doesn't argue. That sometimes makes me wonder whether they share stuff with each other. Were they like that back then too?"

She looks at me for a moment and then starts speaking.

"As I said, your parents are the *best* couple I have ever known. A love like that is so rare. At first, I thought maybe everyone is like that in the beginning. And then eventually, it will start to fade. That's how it is in most relationships. But when I see them now, it is just as it was back then. Nothing's changed. They haven't changed a bit. I can't believe it either. I mean yeah, they used to fight and argue a lot. Some days, they even went without talking. But it was never to a point where they couldn't stand each other. They always found a way to reconcile. They just couldn't be apart. And if you think that your parents don't share stuff with each other, you are wrong. They do. They still have disagreements and fights. They just did a great job at hiding it from you. As they should. Children should never be involved in parents' issues. They always make sure you are happy. And they are happy too, considering they have an amazing daughter. They are the best parents too," she says, stroking my hair. I smile. She looks the other way when she says, "The day you were born, I was the happiest person on earth. Probably more than your parents. I never left your side. Your parents were more than okay to leave you in my care. I remember telling your mother that you are my daughter too. I said, "She is perfect. Just like her mother. Thank you for bringing her into this world. I will make sure to love her more than you guys." She laughs when she finishes the sentence. But I can feel her being saddened. It's so unfair that a warm-hearted person like her can't have children.

"I love you just as much I love my mom, Aunt Ivy," I say, squeezing her hand. She lets out a relieved sigh with a smile and says, "I may be your godmother, but I am no less than a mother. To me, you are my sweet daughter. I don't care about what others think." She looks at me when she says that. No matter how much I wanted to let her know how glad and blessed I am to have her in my life, I just can't bring myself to make up the words.

"Of course. But if she calls you mom too, that would be weird. If you know what I mean," my dad says. We both wince and look at him standing behind us.

"Very funny, Jamie." He chuckles.

"How long have you been standing there?" She asks.

"Right when you were talking about Lily's birth." He looks at the album and goes, "I can't believe you had this all this time." He flips a few pages and halts at a picture where he and my mom are admiring the snow. "Where are the wedding pictures?" He asks. That's when I realize that I have never seen their wedding pictures. There is not one picture of my parents before or of the marriage.

"William probably has them. I haven't had a chance to ask him."
That's weird.

My dad stares at her and doesn't speak. She looks away and says, "It's just that, he's been going on various business trips. He comes back for a few days and heads back again. And he is probably exhausted from all of it. So, I didn't really bother him."

"Okay, I believe you," he says and leaves. She doesn't react. I can see her eyes flicker as she tries to hold back her tears. I feel terrible for her. The fact that she had to endure whatever it was and act like everything was okay seemed like an adult way to avoid trouble. Which by the way, is the stupidest thing an adult can do. Before I could talk, she gets up and says, "We should go back out there." I nod and follow.

~~~

It's been an hour and people are still goofing around in my house. Uncle Simon and Lydia, for whom we arranged this party, are nowhere to be seen. My parents are in the kitchen with Aunt Ivy doing God knows what. My parents didn't want me there. And I am stuck in the living room with a bunch of people I barely know. Which reminds me, I haven't seen Kelly for a while now. And I don't see Gavin either. Maybe they took off together. Just as I get up, I hear a voice say, "You sure stare a lot." His voice makes me flinch all the time.

"I wasn't staring. I was just deep in thought."

"Same difference," Liam says. I sigh. Because it makes sense. But a sudden realization hits me, and I say, "What are you still doing here, by the way? This isn't your cup of tea." He doesn't respond. "I mean, you are not a party person.And clearly, you don't have company."

"I have you." And now, I am the one not responding.

"Clearly, you don't have a company either. So, I am willing to accompany you," he says and smiles.

What was that? He was just being nice. No biggie.

Why does it seem like a big deal though?

"So, what was this party for anyway?" He asks. I realized that not everyone must have known the occasion. People just love parties that they don't care *why* the party is held.

"Uncle Simon and Lydia got engaged. It was a last-minute decision to have this party. As a small celebration, for their engagement. But the list of people to show up was all Kelly's doing. And now I can't find her."

"I saw her leave. Just a few minutes ago."

She just took off? Maybe something happened.

"Thanks for letting me know," I say.

"Don't mention it. By the way, when do we start?"

"Start what?" I ask in confusion.

"Uh, you wanted me to tutor you, remember?"

Ah, yes.

"How about tomorrow?"

"Sounds good. We can start with algebra or geometry. You can choose." I can literally see the excitement on his face when he talks about studying.

"You do know you are a geek, right?" I ask, jokingly.

"Oh yeah," he nods and agrees as if he is proud to be a geek. That makes me laugh.

"Okay, people. Party's over. You can go home now," my mom informs and claps her hand. A few guys sigh and make their way to the door. Liam and I stand up in unison.

My mom approaches us, and Liam says, "It was a great party, Mrs. B."

"That's kind of you, Liam. Thanks for coming," she replies with a smile. Liam then looks at me and goes, "Tomorrow at six," pointing to his wristwatch, and leaves.

"What's tomorrow at six?" My mom makes a questionable face.

"I asked him to help me with my math. He agreed to *tutor* me," I say. My mom's face lit with joy.

Parents express joy for unnecessary stuff.

"That's so sweet of him. How come you never asked him before?"

"I don't know. It never occurred to me until now," I say with a shrug.

"So, you just realized that you suck at math?" She asks with a witty smile.

"Very funny, mom," I fake laugh and fall back on the couch. She sits beside me, and I lean my head on her shoulder. "Where is Uncle Simon, by the way?"

"He went to a tattoo parlour with Lydia." I raise my head to look at her and she goes, "Don't even get me started."

I chuckle. "Did Kelly leave already?" My mom asks.

"Yeah," I nod. "I'll go check on her later. This party was *dull* by the way."

"You're welcome," she teases. We both look at each other and laugh.

"What's so funny?" My dad asks as he makes his way into the living room.

"You," we both say in unison and laugh.

"Well, seems like you guys have finally lost it," my dad says with a laughing nod. Aunt Ivy comes out of the kitchen and says, "I should get going now."

My mom stands up and says, "Okay. Give us a call when you reach home." She nods and smiles. When she leaves, the first thing I do is ask my parents if she is okay.

"She is going through something, isn't she? Did she tell you guys anything?" They look at each other and my dad says, "She thinks her marriage is falling apart. William hasn't been his usual self lately." That for some reason didn't surprise me. The last time I ever saw him with Aunt Ivy was when they came to see my role-play in middle school. And it wasn't all flowers and diamonds back then either. I could tell the difference since I have seen the way my parents were with each other. Of course, not every relationship has the expected happy ending.

But it's sad that not all the best people in the world have it.

14
Sarah

Way back then...

Mr. Richard met with an accident and died when I was fourteen. Of course, he was drunk when he was driving. I couldn't care less.

One down. One more to go. I thought.

But my heart ached for Simon when I realized that he won't have a father. Not that it would have made much difference, but a kid is supposed to grow up with his parents even if it doesn't make any difference. I felt bad for him, for the sole reason that he might be treated differently when people find out he has no father because the world as we all know, sucks.

Nonetheless, I would always be by his side.

The problem was her. She was worse compared to Mr. Richard. And I had to make sure that Simon didn't suffer as I did.

She turned into an alcoholic soon after his death and it just added to our already existing misery. She would drink and throw a tantrum most of the time and I had to be the one to bear it all since I couldn't let her near Simon when she was completely wasted. Most of the time, I would take him to Ivy's and stay there. I would ask her to babysit him, and we were peaceful and happy enough to not let that woman ruin us. However, it wasn't permanent, and I had to take him to that house, to *her*.

She would occasionally check on him in the name of *'love.'* She could *not* fake it more. I kind of understood why she wasn't so good to me but to her own flesh and blood. It was obvious that she thought of us as a burden. And now that her husband was no more in the picture, she could not care less. All she was capable of was making sure our lives were a living hell. Simon wasn't that mature to understand any of it, but it won't be long before he gets a hold of all the things happening around him. There was nothing I could tell him to make him think otherwise. On the other hand, I thought it would be better if he knew everything so that he could make the right decision and free himself from all the crap.

But I had to admit, I was able to do stuff at home I couldn't do before. Like baking. It was one of my favourite hobbies. I had always loved to bake and was never allowed to. But now that the woman was barely sober to notice anything, I did everything I could. At times when she found out, she would nag and leave. It didn't matter anymore since I stopped letting it bother me a long time ago.

~~~

It was a day before Simon's birthday, and I made sure everything was ready for his big party. Ivy was aiding me the whole time and we were so excited for the day. We got Simon a cute bunny outfit and baked him a cake at Ivy's. Her parents were so welcoming and kind. They understood our situation and helped us in every way they could. The party was planned to be held at Ivy's home since it wasn't appropriate at our home with Mrs. Richard being wasted and careless about her own child's birthday.

I left a note on the refrigerator the night before Simon's birthday that read, I would be taking him to Ivy's for his birthday, since talking to her would have been pointless and a waste of time. She would have been too drunk to notice anyway. I had prepared everything beforehand, and I had Ivy come get us since it would be hard for me to carry everything along with Simon. Our homes weren't that far away so it was always easy for us to go back and forth to each other's houses.

Once we reached her home, Ivy's mom approached us with a huge smile on her face and took Simon from me. "Aww you sweet little thing," she said as she swung him from side to side. Simon was cooing and seemed comfortable. He's been here a lot and got attached to everyone here more than his own mother. It was a good thing. *Really good.*

Their idea for the theme for the party was, well, cartoons. And the cake was baked in the shape of a mickey mouse. The only thing left to do was to decorate the house and go with the plan. We had to rest for the night and Simon had to be put to sleep early. Ivy's mother laid him in the bassinet.

"This was Ivy's when she was a kid," her mother admitted. "Glad we still have it for our little Simon here," she smiled and cupped his face. I liked the way she was with him. Like how a mother would be with her child. He seemed happier with these people and that made me happy. I was afraid he would never experience stuff like this but thanks to Ivy, that was not the case.

Finally, in the evening, everyone arrived for his party. There were more kids than I expected. Ivy had our classmates bring along kids from their neighbourhood so that it would be fun. They were playing around and seemed happy. Simon was still napping so we didn't bother to wake him and were waiting for him to wake up on his own. Everything was ready. The cake, the people, the vibe. The only thing left to do was to dress Simon up in his bunny outfit and that probably wouldn't take long, so we waited while the rest of them were occupying themselves with fun games and stuff.

"Sarah! I need you," Ivy called out from the kitchen. I saw her decorating the cake and she wanted me to write the birthday message on it. We planned to do it with chocolate syrup and rainbow sprinkles. I somehow managed to write '*Happy Birthday Munchkin*' on the cake without a flaw. "You know, if we ever had a calligraphy class, you would top it." I smiled.

I could. I thought.

We went back to the living room with the cake in my hand and the next thing I know, the cake was on the floor, completely ruined.

A hand grabbed my hair with such force. It all happened so fast, I couldn't even see or tell who it was until I heard her voice.

"How dare you bring my child here, you little bitch!" she yelled. She reeked of alcohol but was clearly steady enough to throw a tantrum and make a scene, again. "Where is he? Where is my *son*?" she dragged me by my hair through the room and pushed me. I hit my head on the table and got a gash on my forehead. The pain was unbearable, and I couldn't hold myself up. Ivy and her mother came running to me and tried to suppress the blood from my wounded head.

Meanwhile, Mrs. Richard took Simon from the room while he was still asleep and limp in her arms. I was conscious enough to know that he was being taken and that she made a whole lot of mess in front of all these people. It was so embarrassing and hurtful to even think about it, but most of all, I was furious. Her words kept replaying in my mind while I was being taken to the ER. 'Where is my son?' Her *son*? She had no right to call him her son. If she even had the slightest love for him, she wouldn't have done what she did. Even if she hated me so much, it doesn't justify her actions toward her son. I hoped he didn't remember any of it. He was asleep throughout the incident anyway and he would not have this memory even if he was awake, so I was relieved. But it did hurt me to know I couldn't do this for him. The day that was supposed to be his best day was shattered because of me.

Actually, no. His day was ruined because of that woman. That woman would have the worst influence on him, and he would never be happy if she stayed near him.

I would never let that happen. Ever.

15
Jamie

—◦♡◦—

Back then...

Sarah and I decided to move in together right after my local music concert, which was held in central park. I may not be world-famous, but I was at least city famous, and that was enough to sustain my life. We shifted to a new apartment since we had to live together, and it wasn't just her and me. It was her brother, Simon as well. As much as I was excited about the move-in, she was kind of doubtful since she thought I would be uncomfortable with her brother living with us. But little did she know, I loved that kid just as much she did, and we always had a great time together. And if I am not wrong, he felt the same way about me, considering how comfortable and happy he was around me.

I could not wait for us to become a family. I didn't care if that seemed too quick. I had gotten used to them being around so much that I just cannot imagine my life without them in it.

We had planned to take a few of her furniture and home appliances and sell the rest since I had a few myself. We used the money left out of insurance of our parents and the money from selling her house and managed to get a new apartment and the necessary items. We made sure to get a place close to Simon's school. We got a whole place with two floors. We planned to turn the ground floor into a bakery so that Sarah can finally do what she always wanted. I was so excited for her since it was the first time, she did something for herself and I did everything I could to support her. She deserved to live her life the way it should be lived.

And we had our little sweet home on the floor above. It was a three-bedroom house and one of them was allotted to Simon. Out of the other two rooms, one was our room, and the other was turned into a music studio for me so that I could spend time on my music, writing songs, and rehearsing them.

We had Ivy and William help us with the shifting and all the other chores. Not to mention their 'non-platonic' relationship. I don't even know when they started dating and the fact that they grew close in a short time had me astonished since William wasn't the kind of person to easily bond with. It took us almost a year and a half to bond and become friends. And he wasn't that good with women. Never had a serious relationship. Well, I can't be the one to judge since I never had one either, until Sarah. But I knew him better than anyone and he was very different from how I was when it came to any kind of relationship. However, I was glad to see him like that with Ivy.

It was like she brought out the best in him and changed him into a different person. Or rather, a *better* person.

All was done and set, and it was a Friday night, so we decided to have a hangout at *our* new home. The girls were in the kitchen making dinner while I, William, and Simon were in the living room, playing board games. The first was snakes and ladders. Simon was pretty good at it whereas William was wacky. I, on the other hand, was neither here nor there. I did just enough to stay in the game. It was always fun playing children's games. The next game was Jenga. Right around that time, the girls came back with delicious food and joined us for a game of Jenga. Surprisingly, Sarah and Simon were pros at it. The rest of us gave up and it was a face-off between them.

"If I win, I get a new PlayStation," Simon said.

"Deal. But if you lose, no chocolates for a week," Sarah claimed. Simon hesitated before saying, "Fine. We have a deal." They shook hands and proceeded with the game, it was Sarah's turn and she nailed it. Of course.

That's my girl. I thought.

The game got so interesting that we all watched in silence as Simon made his next move. Shockingly, he did a great job. The pile was almost at a collapsing stage and yet, Sarah made the move smoothly. Simon was again in a tough spot.

He had to wait and visualize the outcomes before making his move. For a kid, he was so patient and determined. He finally decided to do it after a long hard consideration and bang! He failed.

"Good game, little brother," Sarah admitted and ruffled his hair. He didn't seem upset about losing though. He was clearly worried that he wouldn't get chocolates for a week. That for him was worse than not getting a PlayStation. But now that he had neither, it was way worse.

"Also, as per the bet, no chocolates for a week," she reminded. He nodded. "Instead—," she began and that caught his attention. I was waiting for her to complete whatever she was going to say. But she stood up and walked to our room. We stared at each other, not knowing what was going on and when she returned, she had a box. The sight of the box made Simon jump with excitement. He grabbed the box and exclaimed, "Whoa!"

I did not see that coming. She had to have planned this way before. She clearly knew how to cheer people in the least possible situation. The smile he had on his face after receiving it was priceless.

"Well, what do you know? You get the PlayStation and a week's free of bakery products," Ivy declared. "Of course, after the bakery's officially opened."

He looked from Ivy to Sarah and finally said, "How did I get a sister like you? There is no way I am this blessed." He delivered it like a sarcastic comment, but clearly meant what he said. She smiled and the next thing we know, they were hugging. He said thank you in a muffled voice and she patted him in a way that said, '*what are sisters for.*'

"Wow, you guys have the best sibling chemistry," William admitted. "I envy you guys." At that, Ivy rubbed his arm and said, "Well, you and Jamie are pretty close like brothers, right?" He shrugged and said, "Yeah, well."

"Oh, yeah. We *are* brothers, aren't we, Will?" I said in a teasing tone and locked arms with him. He immediately unlocked it and went, "Am good," and took a bite of his sandwich, clearly annoyed with the situation. That made us laugh.

We called it a night after a great chit-chatting and hangout session. William and Ivy took off and Simon went straight to bed, all exhausted and satisfied. Finally, it was me and her in a quiet and peaceful space. We were sitting on the swing placed on the balcony. She had her back to my chest, and we were covered in one blanket, snuggling, and enjoying the night view.

"I can't believe we actually made it this far," she admitted. At that, I kissed her on the side of her head and responded, "I can. I was waiting for this to happen, and I was sure that this would happen someday."

I couldn't see her face, but I could feel her sighing with a relieved smile. I pulled her closer to me and gave her a quick peck on the cheek.

"How did you know we would be endgame?"

"I just did."

"I mean like, what if it doesn't work out between us in the future?"

I didn't answer her right away. I knew it would definitely work out between us, but I didn't want to come out too strong and make her think it was forced in any way.

"If it doesn't work out, I will make it work. No matter what happens, I will make sure we do our best to make ourselves worth it, whether or not we are together." She turned to me and smiled. "I hardly doubt that we won't end up together, by the way," I said. "We are destined."

"How can you be so sure?" she asked.

I kissed her ear, "Because—," and whispered, "*we belong.*"

16
Lily

Present day

It's over a week and Kelly hasn't been to school. Nor did she contact me after leaving the party uninformed the other day. When I went to check on her, her mother said that she had left for her grandmother's place. But something didn't seem right. She would have told me if she were to go to her grandma's. It was so unlike her to not talk to me for over a week. So, I decided to stop by her place again to check for myself. She is troubled by something, and I wonder why she isn't telling me.

I am walking down the street which is close to her house and suddenly a car comes to halt beside me.

"It *is* you." His voice makes me squirm.

"Hi, Gavin. What are you doing here?" I ask and instantly feel stupid.

What an obvious question. He must be here to see Kelly as well.

"I was just passing by. I saw you from a distance and figured it would be you. Hop in. I will drive you," he says and smirks.

Gosh, that smile.

I hate myself to think this. I stand there, not realizing I haven't responded to him.

"Yeah, okay. Thanks," I say and get in the car. Instant regret rushes through me and I do everything to distract myself. I look out the window and try not to seem obvious. I know I just got into the car, but it feels like it will take hours before we reach, even though it will take less than ten minutes to Kelly's house.

"So, where are you headed to?" he says, looking at me.

"Uhm...to Kelly's."

"Oh. Okay."

Okay? That's it? Did they have a fight? Is that why he isn't saying much?

"Aren't you headed there as well?" I ask.

"What? Why would I?"

Okay, WHAT?

"Wait a minute. Aren't you guys dating?"

He lets out a laugh and says, "No! What made you think that?"

Is he serious right now?

"The fact that you two were seeing each other. That's called dating," I say, firmly. "Were you just goofing around with her?"

"Whoa, hey. I never said it was exclusive. Hell, I never even told her I was into her. She assumed and made a fool of herself," he says matter-of-factly. "By the way, you were the one I wanted to see," he says and slides his hand down my thigh. I am just too stunned to react to it right away. At the same time, I am filled with disgust that it makes me want to puke. All I can think about is breaking his arm like a twig.

"Get your filthy hand off me," I say in the politest tone possible. That makes him look at me with confusion. "What? Oh, I bet no girl has ever said that to you. Now pull over."

He doesn't respond, nor does he stop the car. I just couldn't keep cool. "Pull over, now!"

And then he does. I don't even wait for the car to come to a complete halt. I open the door to get out and slam it as hard as I can. I walk away when I hear him say, "Your loss!" And then I do the most obvious thing, done by almost every other person in such circumstances. I show him the finger without turning back.

~~~

I rang her doorbell twice and she shows up at the third. She was in her PJs and looked dull.

"God, you're a mess," I say. "Why didn't you just tell me?" At that, she looks flustered.

"Tell you what?" she asks.

"I know, Kel. I just met that jerk. I can't believe he did that to you. What an *ass*!" I yell and emphasize on the last word. She still looks confused and says, "What happened? Did he tell you something?" I kind of feel guilty even though it wasn't my fault that he made a pass at me. But I did want to tell her the truth. So, I make sure she is seated and tell her everything in one go as she listens to me blandly. For a while, she doesn't speak. I am afraid she is mad at me but the next thing she says is, "That piece of shit!" and that makes me relieved.

And then she hugs me and says, "I am sorry I didn't tell you. I just felt so stupid to actually believe he was being genuine. And I feel even worse now that I know he hit on you." I can tell she is regretting it. Who wouldn't? I mean, we all had a crush on that guy but the fact that he turned out to be a complete man-whore makes me cringe. His good looks clouded our judgment.

"Still, how could you not come to school and stay like this? He is not even worth it. What did you tell your parents?"

"I just told them I was sick and that I needed some time alone. They didn't question me much. They just let me be. They're cool," she says with a sigh. And then she says, "God, how did I end up like this? Am so stupid!"

"Hey, c'mon it's not our fault that he is a walking-talking red flag. We just missed seeing it." And now, I sigh. We sit there in silence for a few minutes until my phone pings. I get a text from Liam.

Liam: Tonight at 6?

I had forgotten about the study plan with everything that's been going on. I text him back with a thumbs up and tell Kelly about it. She says, "When did you guys—," she cuts off and goes, "Never mind. Go on. I'll be fine, thanks to you." She gives me a reassuring smile and then I head to my home.

~~~

When I reach home, I see an elderly woman sitting in front of our building. I approach her and ask her if she is lost.

"Does Sarah live around here?" She asks. I am not sure I have seen her before and neither has my mom ever mentioned someone like her. So, the next thing that comes out of my mouth is, "How do you know my mother?" Her smile widens when I say that.

"You're all grown up," she says cupping my face. "It's so nice to see you, dear." I stand there in confusion until she makes herself clear.

"I used to work for your mother in her bakery. This bakery," she says pointing to our building. I knew the ground floor was ours, but I didn't know it used to be a bakery.

My mother's bakery? There is no billboard or any sign of this being a bakery. I wondered why this floor was always empty. Now I know.

I finally speak up and say, "We live upstairs. Let me take you to her." I lead her to my home and when my mom sees her, she comes and hugs her.

"Oh, my god. It's so nice to see you again, Aunty Rose," my mom says.

"Likewise, dear. How have you been doing?" she says, tucking a strand of my mom's hair behind her ear.

"Really well," she says, giving out a laugh. Meanwhile, I just stand there not knowing what or how to react. But then she turns to me and says, "You are probably wondering who I am. I am disappointed that your mother never mentioned me to you. But now that am here, I want us to acquaint ourselves. What do you say, dear?"

I smile and nod. Because I do want to get to know her.

I kind of like her already.

"Let's take a walk, shall we?' she asks. I nod and head out with her.

We are passing by a park, and she takes a moment before talking. I am assuming she is about to say something that needs me to brace myself as well, so I do and wait for her to start.

"Back in the day, I worked at your mother's house for a very long time as a maid. Sometimes a babysitter. I have known your mother ever since she was a kid. Of course, she was adopted, which I presume you already know."

I nod again. I did know that. I knew she was adopted, and that Uncle Simon is not her actual brother. Not that it made them any less of a family. And it absolutely didn't seem to bother any of us. But that is all I know. And the fact that my mom's adoptive parents died when she was a teenager. I have never asked much about them, and mom never really mentioned them, so I didn't bother. But I would like to know more now, and I don't know if my mother would let me in on all her stories.

She heads towards the park, so I follow her. She takes a seat on a bench near the swing set where a lot of kids are laughing and playing. I take a seat next to her and wait for her to continue. She looks at those kids and goes, "I don't have children of my own. So, I have always loved kids a lot and wanted to be around them. Sarah was one such kid and my most beloved. I bonded with her in a way I have never bonded with any other children. It was probably because she was never cherished by her adoptive parents the way she should've been. I knew the moment I saw her that she was a brilliant and precious soul. She would always spend her time with me since her parents never made time for her. And I was the happiest when I was with her playing, talking, and sometimes cooking. She helped me in the kitchen from time to time and she was so good at baking. That's how she ended up finding her interest in baking."

I cannot believe my mother never told me any of these.

She tells me more of the incidents and stories of how she was treated and how she put up with it, back then. As she keeps going on, it just keeps getting intense and painful. Things I never imagined had happened and all I can do is listen to her with a pitiful expression.

The moment she finishes talking, my heart feels heavy. I find myself in tears and agony. It's like I am stabbed straight through my heart. I can't believe my mother went through so much as a child and yet lives like nothing ever happened. She must have bottled up all her pain and suffered all alone.

"Your mother is the strongest and the kindest person I know," she admits. "She reached out to me when she moved here and started the bakery. I was all alone and had no place to work. So, I moved here just so I could work here and be near her. She is like a daughter to me."

I am still too stunned to talk, and I feel her hand on mine as she says, "I know it's hard to process and this is probably why she never told you any of these and probably never will in the future."

I somehow manage to let the words out of my mouth this time. "Then why did you tell me? What if mom finds out and confronts you or something?"

"Because you should know how your mother lived her life. Although, I don't know much. This is just the gist of what happened to her. I was asked to leave, and God knows what she has been through ever since then. You should know her pain and suffering just so you never take her for granted. Your mother literally lives for you. She shut down the bakery because she wanted to focus on raising you and spending the maximum time with you. She wanted to give you what she never received, which is everything. But most importantly, love."

I know my mother is the only person who would do literally anything for me, but it isn't fair to her to not do what she loves just for the sake of me.

"Speaking of which, if Sarah ever asked about what we talked about, don't let her know about this conversation and feign ignorance." I nod. Because now I know why she never told me any of these and I don't blame her. But I also don't think that it's right for her to stay like this now.

I wonder if dad knows any of this. What about Uncle Simon? Or Aunt Ivy? Maybe she never told anyone and suffered all alone.

My thoughts are interrupted by a ball at my feet. The kids shout and ask me to pass the ball back to them. I do the same and then we make our way back home. I try my best to not let my thoughts and worry show on my face as we meet our mom.

"Hey, guys. So, you guys had fun bonding?" She asks with a huge smile on her face. The moment I see her smile, I almost break down and my mom being my mom says the next obvious thing.

"You okay, sweetie? What did you—" I cut her off with a hug and say, "You should open the bakery again, mom. Please! I hate the fact that you never told me about it and now you are wasting your time and dream. I am all grown up now so you should focus on your dream now!"

I can't believe the words that came out of my mouth, but I am sure Aunty Rose wouldn't mind me telling these, since it doesn't concern any of the other things, she told me. I glance at her just to be sure and she gives me an assuring smile. But I still can't stop thinking about all the other stuff she told me. My mom pulls away just enough to see my face and says, "Okay, I will."

I am surprised and happy at the same time when I say, "For real?"

"Oh, yeah. My daughter wants something from me, and I can never refuse her." That makes me smile but also, not what I want.

"Mom, I want you to do it for *you*. Not for me. I know you love baking. You gave that up for me, whom you also love. No one could ever love me as much as you do but please don't ever give up on things you love for the sake of me. I don't want to see you sacrifice the things you love for the other love you have."

Wow. Did I just say those lines?

My mother embraces me this time with all she has and says, "Oh, you really have grown, my beautiful baby," with a shaky voice. She almost teared up and now I had to make her feel better.

"I am so happy I finally got to see the two of you," Aunty Rose conveys. We turn our attention to her and then realize we are standing in the living room with different expressions.

"Aren't you ladies hungry?" I hear my dad call from the kitchen. I didn't know he was here. "And by the way, I agree with Lily. You should reopen the bakery, babe. People miss your pastries," he says walking into the living room. At that, she gives out a small laugh.

"Come on, let's have dinner," my mom says and leads us. I get a text and when I look at my phone, I realize I completely forgot about the study session with Liam.

Liam: Is it still on?

I look at the time and it's seven minutes past six. I send him a quick text while letting my parents know that I will be home late after the study session, and I don't give them time to respond. I grab my bag and rush to the front door and leave in a hurry.

~~~

I see him waiting outside the café with a black tee shirt and a pair of pale blue jeans, with some of his messy strands of hair in the front, almost covering one of his eyes. He has no bag or notes whatsoever. But seeing him waiting for me outside made my heart flutter. Although, it was nothing. But he could've waited inside the café, but he didn't. Maybe it was seeing him in his unusual but cool outfit or the fact that he agreed to help me and is waiting for me out in the cold or that he looks impeccable. My mind was filled with all those thoughts about my mom but seeing him waiting for me made me feel light. He is just the distraction I need.

I stand there, lost in my thoughts when he approaches me and takes the bag from me. "I almost thought you wouldn't show up to our very first session," he says and heads inside the café. I forgot his voice was so deep and enticing. I snap out of my ridiculous thoughts and head inside. He was seated in the second last booth, facing me. I pace faster and sit across from him. The moment I sit, a waitress comes with two butterscotch milkshakes and says, "It's on the house. Enjoy!" with a huge smile.

I look at him, flustered, and before I could, he says, "That's my sister. She is excited that I am here with a girl for once."

She was his sister? And he has never been here with a girl?

I turn to look at her and she is already smiling at us. I give her an awkward smile and turn to him.

"How did you know I like butterscotch?"

"It's my favourite flavour. And Jenna just brought it thinking you wanted to try it as well."

We both like butterscotch. What are the chances?

I turn again to see Jenna and mouth 'thank you', holding the glass. She gives me a wink and vanishes into the staff's room. "She is sweet," I say, turning back to him.

"Yeah, she is. To everyone but me." I chuckle. I envy people having siblings. Their relationship is something unique, that only they have and know.

"So, where should we start? Algebra? Geometry?" he asks, taking a sip of his milkshake.

"Geometry. It sounds easier." At that, he gives out a chuckle. "You're gonna get disappointed, L," he says, shaking his head with a tight-lipped smile.

~~~

After an hour or so, we finally head out of the café. Liam and his sister are talking at the entrance while I stand out and wait for him. I see him giving his sister money. It must be for the milkshakes, but she refuses it. He comes back and she yells, "Have fun, guys!"

We both look at her and Liam says, "We will!" And now, I look at him. He immediately says, "Sorry about that. She does this thing where she makes people uncomfortable."

"I wasn't uncomfortable. I mean, I was in the first few moments, yeah, but she is cute. I like her. She wouldn't even let you pay for the shakes. That is a perfect sister."

"She wants me to buy her a pair of boots for all the free stuff she has given me. Which is why she didn't take the money. I never wanted it free. It's just her way of negotiating."

"Wow," I say with a laugh. "I did not see that coming."

"Yeah. She is unpredictable. But a great support. She is the reason for this makeover," he says, gesturing to himself.

"Oh, yeah. I wanted to ask you about that. You were this nerd-looking guy in school, with glasses and not-so-messy hair. Now you look like a whole other person thanks to your sister."

"Yeah, I get that a lot. That's why I owe her."

"Makes total sense," I nod.

We walk in silence for a while and then Liam breaks the silence with, "By the way, are you coming to the Catskill mountains?"

"Where?" I ask with confusion.

"Hiking. The school trip?" He says it like a question.

"Oh, my god! For real? Camping?" I jump with excitement.

"Yeah. Didn't you know? The guys in our class somehow managed to convince Mr. Hudson to ask permission and here we are."

"When are we leaving?"

"Next weekend."

"Yay! This is so exciting." I cannot stop smiling. I feel like a kid who is in Disneyland. Maybe because I have never been on an actual school trip that was a two-days-one-night kind of trip. And it's camping. Kelly is going to be super excited as well.

"Well, aren't you a cutie," I hear him say.

He just called me a cutie.

To that, the words that come out of my mouth, to my surprise are, "What did you say?" I don't know why I asked that when I clearly heard what he said. But him being him, he responds with, "You were cute just now. Hence, cutie."

Damn, he is something. I am probably blushing like an idiot.

"We are here," he says, looking over my shoulder. I turn to see that I am in front of my house. I turn back to him and say, "Thanks for walking me home. And for the tutoring."

"Anytime. Oh, and I want those questions solved by tomorrow," he says as he leaves and without turning back, he gives me a wave. And I just stand there, grinning like a pathetic teenager who just found her prince or something.

17
Sarah

Way back then...

It was a bright, sunny day, with birds chirping, mild wind breezing, and Mrs. Richard yelling at the top of her lungs for more booze. She was totally out of control. With her constant drinking and rummaging for more, creating a complete mess out of the house. It was depressing enough to protect her own son from her, and this just added to my burden way more. Forget the fact that she was supposed to breastfeed him. He has not had breast milk ever since Mr. Richard passed away. Basically, he consumed it for at most five-six months, which was very less. I made sure to get him all the necessary supplements and formula while she was getting wasted.

The store I worked at was a hazard for the first few months since the sales weren't that great. I somehow managed and brought up the sales and kept track of all the products and goods that were to be delivered to us. I worked more than the owner. It was like I was the one owning it. I worked my ass off and it paid off. I was now the general manager of the store and had almost the whole control of it.

When I made just enough, I would spend it for Simon and save the rest for the future. I spent very little for myself, enough to survive, and never gave a penny to Mrs. Richard since she would waste it all on alcohol. Besides, she had insurance money. But I don't think she used it much. Maybe she was too drunk all the time to even remember she had it. So, there must be a lot left.

To work and take care of the house was devastating. I couldn't leave Simon alone at home, so, I would take him to the store with me while I worked. The customers would play with him and make him giggle from time to time and that was satisfying to hear. He never seemed to miss his mother. He was always happy when he was with me, so I was relieved.

~~~

The other day, when I was at the counter, attending to a customer, I heard Simon say, "Happy".

Happy. Happy was his very first word. I have read that babies who tend to have keen observations of what they see and hear are gifted. I often said "Happy thoughts" whenever Mrs. Richards threw a fit. I was afraid that with her constant cursing and yelling, Simon might have a bad influence, that he would see and learn things he shouldn't. But the first thing he ever learned was the word, 'happy'. That word sounded way more beautiful from his mouth. That sweet little voice and smile when he said it is still afresh in my mind. I could not be happier! This kid deserved the world, and I would make sure he gets everything he wants. I wanted to make sure he grows up to be a man that everyone respects and cherishes.

I started working two shifts and made sure to earn the maximum. Ivy was a great help at times when I needed her to babysit Simon. We all would picnic at times and sleep over most of the time. Simon always seemed happy and healthy, physically, and mentally. And that's all I ever wished for.

It worked. And it will keep working in the future. For sure.

18

Jamie

⸱♡⸱

Back then...

"Will you be my constant forever?" I asked, bending on one knee, with a ring in my hand and a huge smile on my face, waiting to hear the words from her. Seconds started to feel like hours, but she finally replied with a huge yes and knelt before me, so we were at the same level and said, "For eternity," and kissed me. The kiss lasted for like a minute and then I put the ring on her finger and finally yelled, "We're engaged!" off the top of my lungs. I could let the whole world know that Sarah Richard was going to be my wife!

William and Ivy came running to us and hugged us.

"God, this is so overwhelming. In a good way. I am so happy for you guys!" Ivy said, teary-eyed.

"Hell, you guys are gonna make a great couple for life!" said William. We were so happy we couldn't stop feeling this overwhelming joy and excitement. We just couldn't wait and freaked out.

"Let's get married right now!" I said swiftly. Everyone's eyes were on me, and I couldn't care less. All that mattered was that I was so deeply and ridiculously in love with her that I just wanted to marry her right away.

While those two were going on about how it was way too soon and that we needed a plan or something, she replied with, "Okay. Yeah, we should totally get married right now."

"What? Sarah, come on. What about the big wedding plans and stuff? You can't just get married out of the blue," Ivy demanded.

"Guys, she is right. You guys are engaged now, so there is no need to rush," William sided with her.

"Yeah, but this moment is what matters. We want to remember the exact moment at which we got married. This feeling, this excitement, this rush of adrenaline. It feels right. Who cares about the place and time when it feels just right? It's the perfect time to get married," Sarah said in reply.

They couldn't come up with anything else to object to that. And I was speechless as well. I did suggest that we get married right away but after hearing what she said, I could not wait another second. I carried her in my arms and headed to the nearest church.

"You guys meet me at the church with the rings and other wedding stuff in an hour!" I yelled as I was making my way forward with her smiling in my arms and wrapping her arms around my neck.

"Rings? Where do I get the rings at the last moment?" William shouted.

"Sounds like a groomsman problem," I reverted.

~~~

An hour later, they were here with the dress and the rings and a photographer.

"We found a last-minute photographer. You're welcome," William said with a nudge.

"Thanks, bud," I said, patting him.

"Here's your dress, girl. This is so not the one I wanted you to wear. But this is what I could find at the last minute. But the dress is blue and new. I bought it so it could be 'your something blue' and 'something new'." Ivy gave her the dress with much less enthusiasm.

"Hey, you have no idea how happy I am with this dress. The fact that you got me this dress right now, even though we rushed it, is all that matters. Thanks a ton. I love you," Sarah admitted.

"I love you too, S," she hugged her. "Oh, and here," she said handing her a hairpin that had a flower made of rubies and white stones, "This could be your 'something borrowed' and 'something old'."

"Oh, my god. That's so cute," Sarah said and wore it on her hair.

"Do we have a priest yet?" William asked.

"Oh, about that. Can you be the one to wed us? I mean, I know I have already troubled you with the groomsman duties, so I know it's a lot to ask of you—,"

"Are you kidding me, Brooks? Of course, I would do it. It'd be my honour," he cut me off. I smiled and nodded.

After a few minutes, she came in wearing the not-so-wedding-y but perfect dress and all I could think was, *'How did I even get her? I've got to be the luckiest person right now.'*

I extended my hand and pulled her closer to me. "You look like you're gonna be my wife." At that, she chuckled and replied, "I can't wait," with a wink.

"So...since it's just the four of us and the fact that you guys are in a hurry to get married, shall we just skip the vows and go straight for the rings?" William asked.

We both nodded. "Yeah, we already told everything we needed to say to each other ever since we met and fell in love. We can do the rest after the wedding, can't we now, babe?"

"Hell yeah!" she exclaimed. I grinned.

"Jamie? Do you take, Sarah, as your lawfully wedded wife and promise to stay together, in sickness and in health, till the very end?"

"I do."

"Sarah? Do you take, Jamie, as your lawfully wedded husband and promise to stay together, in sickness and in health, till the very end?"

"I do," she said with the sweetest smile.

We exchanged our rings, which by the way, was a great choice for a couple's ring. I gave him a look that said, "Good job with the rings,

Will." He certainly understood because he nodded with a wink that meant, "Right backatcha!"

"Okay...then, I pronounce you, man, and wife. You may kiss the brid—," I cut him off by pulling her to me and kissing her without letting him finish the sentence.

"I love you, Mrs. Brooks," I whispered in her year.

"For eternity, Mr. Brooks."

19

Lily

Present day

This was like the seventh day of tutoring, and he makes it easier and more fun for me to understand concepts with his simple explanations and methods. I might score well in math this time, thanks to him. But it wasn't just the tutoring I enjoyed. The fun part was mostly just spending time with him. Being in his presence made me forget the stuff about my mom. It was blissful. I was completely myself and cheerful around him. And so was he. With his jokes and comments at times that made me laugh, his eyes, his voice...I could go on. The point is, he changed me into this crazy lover girl with his charisma. I never felt this way with anyone else before. Not even Gavin. With him, it was just the looks that made me and almost the entire school drool over. But turns out, he was a huge A-hole and I hate him for what happened with Kelly.

Liam, on the other hand, is the exact definition of a man. I know he is a teenager, but he is more of a man than any man I have met. Well, except for my dad. My dad had eyes only for my mom and that's how a man should be. Although, I don't know that well about Liam. From the looks of it and from the time I have spent with him, he seems to be the ideal type that I am imagining. I sincerely hope he is.

We have been hanging out at the café, his home, and my home from time to time. Right now, we are in his room, and I am sitting on the floor with my back to his bed. He is at his desk, correcting my assignment and his expression tells me I did well. A few minutes pass and he comes and sits next to me on the floor with something in his hand.

"I am really proud of you, L," he says and hands me a chocolate bar. I laugh and take it.

"Actually, you should be proud of yourself to have made me this better."

"You know what? You are absolutely right," he agrees and takes the chocolate back. I laugh again. I can't seem to react any other way when being around him.

He takes a bite of the chocolate and hands it to me. "You all set for tomorrow?" he asks.

"I take a bite of the chocolate and say, "Oh, yeah. Am way too excited that I don't think I can sleep tonight."

"You must love trips." He takes the chocolate bar from me.

"Of course. Don't you?"

"Not much of a fan."

"Oh, that's right. I forgot you are a nerd." When I finish the sentence, I notice the guitar he had when he was at my dad's store. I go and pick it up. "This is so cool," I say and play a little tune from the song, 'Lover' by Taylor Swift.

Oh, by the way, I am a huge Taylor Swift fan.

"Wow, that is good. You know how to play?" he asks curiously.

"Just a tad. My dad does it often, so I just pick a few and play at times. But you can. Very well. Can you play something?" I ask, handing him the guitar. He takes it from me and says, "Sure. Name a song."

"The one I just played."

"What was it?"

Seriously?

"You're kidding, right? How can you not know Taylor Swift?" I ask him with genuine shock.

"Oh. I don't listen to her songs," he says and starts playing 'Until I Found You', by Stephen Sanchez.

Yes. I know other artists as well.

"Dude, how can you—" I scoff. "Well, now I am disappointed."

"Hey, I can play if I hear the song once. What song is it?"

"Nah, it's okay. Don't bother. From what I just heard; you play damn well. But I am still disappointed."

He laughs and keeps the guitar down. He slowly comes closer to me and walks past me as if I wasn't just standing there. Then, he swiftly swirls me around and grabs me by the waist. I am too stunned to react, and he quietly says, "I can't have you disappointed in me."

He lets me out of his grip, and I just stand there, all perplexed and flushed.

"Lily?" he calls out. I turn to see that he is standing at the doorway, waiting for me.

"Oh, right. Yeah, sorry," I say and pace quickly. As we reach his front door, his sister pops out from the living room and says, "Hey, guys. So, did you guys have fun at math?" I manage to say, "Oh, yeah. It was really fun." And then I glance at Liam and notice that he is smirking.

"Okay...I'll see you tomorrow. Thanks for the session. Good night." I walk out of there so fast that I can't feel my legs. I am not sure if he was just goofing around. After the Gavin incident, I find it hard to trust this kind of stuff. He seems like a good person. But I don't know him for sure. Though, I hope he is the person I think him to be. I wouldn't know until I spend more time with him, but I am worried it might screw things up. It's a fifty-fifty possibility. Probably worth the try, I guess.

~~~

We were all asked to wait for the bus to arrive and we all were more than just excited, although I am a bit sleepy since I didn't get enough sleep last night with all the excitement and the Liam thing. A few of them brought a lot of stuff for a two-day trip. Kelly and I were the only ones with one bag, I guess. I mean you wouldn't need much when you go camping, other than enough energy boosters and blankets.

"Maybe we should have brought a lot of stuff too. Seems like we're the odd ones here," Kelly says.

"Well, we have a camera and other electronic gadgets, so I think we're good to go."

"Electronic gadgets?" she gives out a laugh. "Spoken like a nerd. I guess Liam turned you into one."

His name makes me flinch. And the next moment, I find myself searching for him. I haven't seen him yet.

Maybe he wasn't coming since he said he wasn't much of a fan of trips. Or maybe, he is running late. Or maybe, he is already here and hiding somewhere.

I realize I turn into a pathetic person when it comes to him.

"Okay, guys? The bus is here. We are all set to go," Mr. Hudson informs us.

"Okay...here we go!" Kelly sounds excited. As we walk towards the bus, she halts, and her expression changes. I see what she was looking at, and it made sense. Gavin had his arm around a girl named Linda and I swear to God, all I want is to punch him in the face so hard, that he wouldn't want to be near a girl for months.

"Hey, c'mon. Don't let that perv ruin your fun," I say, giving her a nudge.

"Yeah, you're right. I mean, I am not in the wrong here. So, screw him! Let's have fun!"

"Heck, yeah," I agree and exclaim.

We get on the bus, and I see Liam sitting at the back with his guitar and air pods in his ears. He doesn't notice me. Or anyone, for that matter.

How did he get here so quickly? And when? Well, at least he made it.
I have got to stop.

Kelly takes the window seat and I take the seat next to hers. I turn to look at him, but he is staring at his phone, probably texting someone. I turn my attention back to Kelly, who is busy taking selfies. She locks her arms with mine and clicks a pic. "This is going on my Instagram."

I yawn. "Hey, am gonna get some shut eye. You okay though?"

"Yeah, girl. Sleep tight. I'll wake you when we arrive," she assures me.

"Kay, thanks," I say and close my eyes, not trying to think of anything and letting my mind relax.

~~~

"L, we're here. Wake up!" I hear Kelly's voice. I also hear mumbling sounds around me and when I open my eyes, I see everyone getting down.

"Wow, you slept like a log," she tells me, fixing my messy hair. "Well, now we gotta hike. Let's go!"

I take my bag and make my way toward the door and before I take a step down, my ankle twists, and I almost fall until someone grabs my arm from behind. I turn around thinking it was Kelly but to my surprise, it was Liam. "Uh...thanks," I stutter.

"Anytime," he says, with a hint of a smile. He gets down first and takes my bag from me so that I get down. Kelly follows me and he takes her bag as well.

"Thanks, dude," she tells him. I look at her with a questionable expression which makes her go, "What?"

"*Dude*? When did you guys get so close?"

"Well, we've talked once or twice. He's been in my chem class."

"Well, that's news to me," I say as I walk.

"I didn't think it was a big deal," she says and halts. "Wait a second...are you—?" she pauses and gives me the look. My silence answers her and she goes, "Oh, my god! You serious?"

"It's not what you think. I just—," she cuts me off and says, "Like him?" I hesitate and that confirms her suspicion.

"OMG. You *like* him." She sounds excited.

"I don't even know if I do. It's just...maybe I do. I—"

"Okay, this is amazing. All those tutoring lessons paid off," she grins. "There he goes," she says pointing toward him. "Liam?" She yells. "Hey, Li—" I elbow her.

90

"What are you doing? Look, I don't even know if he feels the same way. Besides, this could just as well be a crush. So, let's not do anything about it. Alright?"

"Roger that," she nods. "But I think this is more than 'just a crush'," she air-quotes and laughs. I shake my head and sigh.

We keep walking and climbing the hill-type path and it's so chilly even though I've covered myself with layers.

I have always wanted to come to the Catskill mountains since it is famous and a great hiking spot. It's basically the Catskill Forest Preserve and the spot we are headed to is the North-South Lake campground. Even though there is a resort and other facilities, we preferred camping because it's adventurous.

We take a few breaks in between and some even take pictures. Kelly does the same. I look around and my eyes fall on Liam, who still had his air pods on and is busy with his phone. He is such a music freak. The fact that he carried his guitar all the way here, confirms it.

"L, smile!" Kelly calls out and when I turn to see her, she clicks a pic. That's going to be one weird pic of mine.

~~~

It is almost dusky, and we finally reach our destination. The place looks incredible. There is nothing but greens. Hills and mountains with chilly air and calm scenery. We gather around and plan on the spot for our tents. Once we decide on the spot, we start setting up the tents. Two people per tent were the plan. So, Kelly and I decided to share one.

We were done with ours so, we look around to see the nearby tents. The tent almost two feet away from ours was Gavin's. Kelly notices it and says, "You know what? This spot isn't that good anyway. Let's switch with someone." I kind of want that too but I don't think anyone would agree to so that.

"You guys can stay in my tent," I hear him say. I fleetly turn to see Liam standing near our tent.

"Really? You wouldn't mind?" Kelly asks.

"Nope. You can have it," Liam assures us and looks at me.

"Were you eavesdropping?" I don't know why that came out of my mouth. That wasn't what I wanted to say. But he chuckles and says, "Not really. But I do know that you guys need to stay as far away from Gavin as possible."

How considerate of him.

Kelly dope-slaps me and says, "Sorry about that, Liam. She has a long way to go. But thank you so much."

"Anytime," he smiles and walks away. That just made my heart skip a beat.

What is he?

"He is so into you," she clarifies. I give her a doubtful look. "Come on, he just did something a boyfriend would do for his girlfriend."

I still doubt it.

"He helped us both. He is just a good, helping person. That's all."

"Yeah right." She does the eyeroll.

We all gather and sit around the campfire, and enjoy ourselves to the fullest. Night and chill vibes, guys cheering and dancing, drinks and snacks, and a fun time with friends. It's the best.

Kelly is chit-chatting and clicking pics while I am sitting there, looking at her making funny faces for the photos. I see Liam with his guitar and playing it. I can't hear what he is playing but I can see he is really into it and looks absolutely gorgeous from my view.

"Hey, Liam? Why don't you play something? You've been on your guitar ever since we started the trip," a guy says. Everybody else starts cheering him to play a song.

"Yeah, sure. Well, I have been practicing this song for someone," he says, looking at me. Just as he does, all eyes are on me, and I can't seem to react.

"Oh. My. God!" Kelly exclaims.

"Whoa," everyone says in unison. I am still too stunned to speak.

"This is exclusively for you, Lily," Liam admits from afar and starts playing.

Is that an open confession?

Everyone goes dead silent and looks at him. The moment he starts, my jaw drops, and my heart flutters because the song he plays is the song I asked him to play a few days ago. The song he claimed he's never heard before. The song that I love. I can't believe he searched and listened to Taylor Swift's 'Lover', just so he could play it for me in front of everyone. Not only is he playing, but he also starts singing it. The lyrics from his mouth, with his voice, sound way too fascinating and beautiful.

No offense, Taylor. I might just as well be in love right now.

Literally, everyone is admiring him, and that kind of feels strange. I know this is my moment and that he is doing this for me. I am overwhelmed with mixed emotions I can't explain. All I want to do is to freeze this moment forever and live in it for the rest of my life. There is no way in hell I'll be able to go back to my normal life after this. This to me, is a fairy tale moment.

When he's done, everyone applauses. Some of the guys tease him while others adore him. Girls are obviously falling hard for him now. But amongst all of this, his eyes are still fixed on me. Although there is a certain distance separating us right now, him looking at me really feels like he is zero feet away from me. I can neither move nor speak.

"Way to go, my man!" someone says, cheerfully.

"He literally confessed to you. In front of everyone! This is so exciting, L!" Kelly seems to be so happy for me. "I didn't know it was this deep. Isn't he wholesome?"

Yeah! He is. Very much so.

And no. I didn't even know he liked me, let alone know if it was deep.

As my thoughts wander, he approaches me and makes my mind go blank.

"That was so smooth, Liam," Kelly tells him, patting him, and leaves us.

"So...was that the right song?" he asks.

Really?

He waits for me to respond but I still can't seem to get the right words to say. "You know, I had to search every one of Taylor's songs to get it right," he continues. "I just heard you play for a few seconds and I gotta say, you delivered it pretty well."

He is appreciating *me* right now. *Wow.*

I finally let myself speak. "Why would you do this for me?"

"I told you. Can't have you disappointed in me," he replies.

Man, he knows how to make a girl blush.

"So that's what you were doing on your phone? Searching for the song?" I can't help but grin. He gives me a tight-lipped nod.

"You could've asked someone."

"Well, yeah. But this way I seem way cooler. Don't you think?" he conveys. That makes me laugh.

"I like the way you laugh," he adds. "And the way you look at me."

"How...how do I look at you?" I question.

He steps closer and whispers, "The way you're looking at me right now." He is so close I can hear him breathe. I never knew someone could make you feel this way. Like the only person you are destined to be with is here, trying to impress you and win you over. Well, it bloody worked.

"Can I kiss you?" he requests. It was too straightforward that I couldn't answer him. But that didn't mean I didn't want it. I so want it.

You know what I find most attractive in a man? *Consent.*

He understood my silence and closed the distance between us. He caresses my cheek with the back of his hand. He then moves his hand to a strand of my hair and tucks it behind my ear. My eyes instantly fall shut when I feel him inches away from me. I steady myself for the next, obvious move, but what he does is beyond my expectation, in a good way.

He gently presses his soft lips against my forehead and stays like that for almost a minute, which by the way felt more like an eternity. I couldn't have asked for a more perfect kiss.

"Dude! That wasn't what we were expecting!" a guy yells.

"Shut up. It was perfect," Kelly argues.

That's when I realize all the eyes watching us. It literally felt as though we were the only ones in this world. Not place, but world. A world of just him and me. That's the dream.

He places his forehead against mine and whispers, "Finally," and embraces me. He holds me tight, and I can feel his heart race. That makes me smile because he is just as nervous as I am. But he is so good at handling the situation, I have got to give him credit for that.

I don't care that people are watching us because this moment is worth it. I would gladly be in it over and over for a lifetime.

~~~

I barely managed to keep it together in the entire trip. It was a memorable day and the fact that am sitting next to Liam on the bus is another memory I would cherish. Kelly had asked Liam to take her place and wanted us to spend more time together.

She is the kind of best friend that everyone needs.

He had his arm around me while I laid my head on his shoulder. He keeps stroking my hair and places quick pecks on my head and cheek from time to time. I just can't get enough of those. I try so hard to stay calm and collected but my reactions and behaviour during Liam's presence are something I can't seem to control. However, I do my best to be nonchalant. But the moment I reach home, I couldn't keep it in any longer.

"Mom!" I call out. "Dad—," my dad cuts me off.

"Whoa, hey! Easy there," he says when I almost bump into him. "How was your trip?" I don't respond. Instead, I keep smiling and that makes him smile as well. "Ooh...what's with the mood?" he nudges me.

"Hey, sweetie," my mom shows up. "How was the trip?"

"I got some news. Sit down." They both look at each other and settle down. They are looking at me, waiting for me to reveal whatever it is that I am about to say.

"You guys know Liam, right?"

"The guitar slash tutor guy?" my dad says it like it's a question. I nod.

"Whoa. Are you two—?" my dad begins. Again, I can't help but smile wide. That answers them.

"But the best part is that...he played me a song. In front of everyone," I say with joy.

"Now that's a man. I approve of him," my dad declares, but in a fun tone.

"He played me my favourite Taylor Swift song!" I exclaim.

My mom laughs and says, "No way! Oh, wow that is so sweet of him." I nod and cover my face.

"Aww, look at you all shy," my dad teases. "He better be worth it."

"Dad? He is one of a kind. Trust me. *And* he is smart. He is the reason your daughter scored well in math."

"Good point."

"I am so happy for you, sweetheart," she squeezes my hand. "You should bring him home sometime. Not as your tutor but as your boyfriend," my mom adds.

"You bet." I smile and give them both a hug. "By the way, I missed you guys."

"I doubt that", my dad reverts in a sarcastic tone.

"Okay, you must be hungry. Let me set the table."

"No, mom I am actually tired, so am just gonna go to bed," I say and head upstairs. I hop onto my bed when I get a text from Kelly.

Kelly: Here's your advance birthday present. You're welcome. XOXO

I play the video she sent and it's of Liam singing the song, with just the perfect lighting and view. I text her back.

Me: OMG. I love you, K!

I connect my air pods, lay down, and listen to him sing. His voice is so soothing that I close my eyes and relive the moment all over again.

20
Sarah

Way back then...

The most precious thing happened when I was at Ivy's with Simon. I was helping Ivy with her assignments and since I wasn't a schooler, it helped me learn as well. Simon was playing with his toys while I was making notes for her essay. Ivy was just about to bring us some snacks when I heard Simon giggle. I turned to see him, and it was just the perfect sight. He was on his two little feet and took his very first step. I stood still and adored every second of it. I could hear Ivy behind me and when she came in, she was just as stunned as I was. We kept watching him fall, crawl, and stand up on his own every now and then. It was the cutest thing to witness, and I was so happy and grateful for his very presence. He was soon exhausted and fell asleep. Ivy had taken a video of him walking for the very first time and treasured it.

He was literally the only thing making me go ahead in my life. And I had to make sure to give him the life he deserved. I was called for a load of pending work, so I had to leave Simon with Mrs. Richard at the house since Ivy was attending her classes and I had to make a few deliveries. She was, as usual, pretty wasted and wasn't aware of him being at home. So, I decided I would make all the deliveries as soon as possible, get all the work done, and reach home.

When I was done, I hurried back home. When I stepped into the house, it was quiet. As I reached the living room, I heard Simon scream and cry from upstairs. I ran up the stairs and went into the room where Simon was. My heart stopped when I saw him on the floor, crying his lungs out, while she had her hands clutched in her hair with an irritated expression.

She kept pacing back and forth. "Shut your mouth, you little shit," she yelled at him. As she neared him, I stepped in front of him.

"Don't you dare," I screamed, and glared at her. I turned to pick him up when she grabbed my hair and yanked me away from him.

"Stay the hell away from my son," she screamed. I grabbed her arm and twisted it enough to let her grip on my hair loosen. I pushed her away from me and said, "This is it. I am done with your shit." I picked Simon up, who was still crying, and walked out of the room. I heard her shouting and following us. So, I turned and said, "You have no right to call him your son. You don't deserve him. Or this life, for that matter. I hope, with all my heart, that you burn in hell." I walked out of the house as fast as I could and shut the door behind me, oh her face. This was the limit. I really had a sliver of hope that she would not hurt Simon. But the fact that she hurt him when she was sober, gave me no choice but to do this. He is no longer safe with her. He was never safe with her, to begin with.

"We can't stay there anymore, buttercup. We are officially moving out of the damned house, away from that evil woman," I said to Simon as I carried him to Ivy's. He was exhausted from all the crying and was limp in my arms. I couldn't help but weep the entire way to her house. I was a bit relieved I had Simon with me even though he was just a little baby. But it wasn't much so, at some point, I had reached my limit. I stopped in the middle of the street, not knowing what to do.

I dropped to my knees and let it all out for good. Since there was no sign of any vehicles or humans around, I held Simon tight in my arms and cried my eyes out for a good whole hour.

21

Jamie

Back then...

I rushed back home when I received the text from Sarah. When I reached home, I saw Ivy and William on the couch, watching Simon make funny faces. When they noticed me, they came running to me saying, "Congratulations, Jamie!" and hugged me. I was still processing it, but the joy was intact, ready to burst out at any moment. I had to see Sarah and know for sure, one last time.

"Where is Sarah?" I asked them.

"She is at the rooftop. Go," Ivy pushed me forward, with a huge excitement on her face. William gave me a thumbs up as I was heading towards the rooftop.

But before I could go up the stairs, Simon grabbed my arm and said, "She was crying. Make sure to cheer her up." He clearly didn't know what was going on, but it was sweet of him to have concerns for her. I carried him on my arms and tousled his hair.

"Your sister is probably crying because she is happy," I assured him. "She is so lucky to have you, Simon," I said and put him down. I ran up the stairs to the rooftop and opened the door, to see her standing near the ledge, with her arms hugging herself. She probably wasn't aware of my presence. I paced to reach her and embraced her from behind. She leaned into me and exhaled a sigh of relief.

I kissed her ear and asked, "Did you double-check? Is it positive?" She nodded and said, "Two hundred percent." I smiled and held her tight. Unbeknownst to me, my eyes teared up and I couldn't hold back. I was so happy I could cry like a baby for all I cared. She turned to me and wiped my happy tears. I placed my forehead on hers and whispered, "Thank you."

"You're going to be an amazing father," she declared.

And a deserving person gets to be a mother. That is everything.

22
Lily

Present day

"Happy sweet sixteen, my beautiful baby girl!" my mom greets me with a huge smile on her face. I am still half asleep when she hops onto the bed and hugs me.

"Thank you, mom," I say, hugging her back. I open my eyes and see my dad leaning against the doorway. He has this smile on his face which indicates, 'you're all grown up'. He walks toward me and says, "Happy birthday, my precious girl." I hug him next and say, "You guys never cease to do this. Every year, you make a big deal out of this. I don't really enjoy birthdays."

"Well, it is a big deal for us. Our only daughter turns sixteen today. That doesn't happen every year now, does it?" my dad argues. *Good point.* I smile and agree.

"So, what do you want for your birthday?" my mom asks. I take a moment before answering.

"I want you to open up your bakery and bake me my birthday cake."

"Atta girl." My dad and I do the high-five.

My mom grins and says, "You got it."

I freshen up and head downstairs to the bakery to see that my mom is wearing her apron and whipping the cream. She looks like a pro patisserie. And not to mention, passionate. She notices me and calls out. Before I go to her, I turn around and flip the closed sign board to open.

I can smell the vanilla from a foot away and it feels like a sweet holiday. My dad comes out of the kitchen with a chef's hat on. That makes me laugh.

"I... just burned the cookies," he says with an awkward expression.

"Jamie!" my mom exclaims.

"Well, technically...the oven burned the cookies," he defends himself with a tight-lipped nod. "They're successfully ruined," he adds. I can't stop laughing. The bell chimes as the door opens and we all look at her as she walks in. My face lightens up when I see her, and I go and give her a hug.

"You finally opened it," Aunty Rose says, looking at my mother. She comes around the counter and gives Aunty Rose a hug as well.

"How did you know—?"

"Lily gave me a call and asked me to come. I can't wait to work here again." She replies. "And...a very happy birthday to you, my dear," she turns to me with a wide smile on her face. Your mother decided to close the bakery for good when you were born. And now, sixteen years later, she decided to open it again on your birthday. It's something special," she declares. I agree with a smile and my dad adds, "Uhm...I can't be happier with your timing, Miss Rose. You are truly a cookie saviour." We laugh and they head to the kitchen to work on it. I let my mom know that I will be upstairs for a while and that she can call me if she needs my help.

I go to my bedroom and check my phone since I haven't seen any of the messages I received. I open it and there are a series of texts. I open Kelly's first.

Kelly: Happy Sweet Sixteen L!! XOXOXO.

She sent a lot of heart and kiss emoticons as well.

The next text I open is of Liam's.

Liam: Happiest birthday to the prettiest girl I know.

Liam: P.S. My girl just turned 16.

That makes me blush and smile ridiculously.

Next is Uncle Simon's text.

Uncle Simon: Happy birthday, my sweet little niece.

Uncle Simon: Lydia sends her hearty wishes as well.

They texted me at twelve. I must be lucky to have such people with me. I text them back with a lot of emojis and gratitude.

~~~

The party started a few minutes ago and almost the entire living room is filled with people. It's mostly my classmates and a few from my neighbourhood. Since my mom opened the bakery, everyone seems to be happy about it. The bakery is officially opened now and will run successfully from tomorrow.

My mom comes in with the cake she baked. It had chocolate frosting with cherries on top. It was a two-layered cake with a lot of rainbow sprinkles on it. It is the perfect cake. She places it on the table, and everyone gathers around as I ready myself to cut it. I see Kelly and Liam standing in front and my parents next to me. These are all the people I need in this moment right now. So, I go ahead and blow the candles after making an obvious wish. I cut my perfect birthday cake, and everyone claps and sings the song. It makes me cringe but also kind of happy for this moment and the people around me.

A few moments later, after receiving all the gifts and greeting, I head towards Liam who is leaning against the front door frame. I look around for my parents but can't place them. So, I ask Kelly to let them know that I am at the rooftop. We head upstairs to the rooftop and lean on the ledge to witness the beautiful night view of the NYC. We don't speak for a while, and he embraces me from behind and kisses the side of my head. For some reason, he smells like lavender, and it is so invasive. "Happy birthday," he whispers into my ears and gives me a soft peck on the cheek. I turn around and say, "Where is my present? You are the only one who hasn't given me my gift yet." He smirks and opens his backpack.

"Before that, I need to go back home soon. I must work on this paper and the deadline is tomorrow."

"Oh, okay," I say with a pout. He cups my face and says, "Sorry. But hey, I have about—," he looks at his wristwatch and says, "fifteen minutes to spare."

"Fifteen minutes? Yay!" I say with a ke excitement. He chuckles and makes me sit on the floor. He takes a seat next to me and hands me the present.

I unwrap it and see a small note that reads, *'My love for you is directly proportional to the sight of you at every second. Well, in simple terms, the more I see you, the more I fall for you. Really deep.'*

I don't look at him, because clearly, he is looking at me and waiting for my reaction. And I think I gave him the one he expected. I can't stop smiling and blushing and my heart's probably pumping blood way too fast than usual, I can feel it in my throat. He tousles my hair and says, "Go on." I do. I open the box and find a few photographs. At first, I can't seem to recognize any of it but when I look closer, I realize that it's a picture of me and Liam from eighth grade. Now it all comes to me. We did this play when were in middle school and that's when we acquainted. I can't believe he still has this picture. There is another picture where it's just me. But it isn't from the play. This was when we were in our freshmen year. The next picture is of Liam. The old Liam with the glasses on and the nerdy look. There was a school yearbook where he circled me and him. And finally, a letter where all that as written was my name followed by a heart.

Oh, my god. Is this what I think it is?

He grabs the letter and says, "Well, I didn't write anything because I wanted to tell you in person someday." I look at him with a flustered expression. "What did you want to say?"

He looks me in the eye and quietly says, "That we are endgame." He cups one side of my face and whispers, "You are mine, Lily Brooks." I let out a huge sigh. Because I honestly don't know what to say or do. I look at photos again. My eyes flicker and mind wander with various thoughts. Most of all, about him. I look back at him and manage to speak. "Liam? Have you been—?" he takes the picture of us during our play and says, "Yep. This is when I fell for you.

Of course, I was just a kid, but it felt real. Like it was meant to be. A permanent bond. I never gave up on you just because of the gut feeling I had. And it worked out for the best. I am glad I followed my heart."

I think I fell hard for him now.

I shake my head and let out a laugh. "Unbelievable. Here I was wondering if you would reciprocate my feeling when you have been doing that for years." I look at him and say, "Is this real?"

He smiles and replies by flicking my forehead. I flinch and he says, "See? It's real."

"I cannot believe it. You have liked me for this long?"

"Nah uh. I have *loved* you." He corrects me. Suddenly, it becomes scorching hot and my heart beats faster again. I feel nervous and become particularly aware of his presence.

He just confessed to me. He loves me. This is probably the best gift I have ever received.

"Lily?" he calls and that snaps me out of my thoughts. I look at him with an apologetic look. "I am sorry, Liam. I didn't know."

"Exactly. You didn't know. There was no way you could've known. I should be the one to apologize."

"No. Why would you? I feel like you've been all alone with all this feeling and no one to share it with." At that, he laughs. I give him a look of confusion.

"I did share it with someone. Jenna. I tell her everything."

"Your sister?" he nods. It all made sense now. Why she treated me like that and why she was happy that he brought me to the café. I can't help but feel sort of proud of him.

"Well played," I say in a way that makes him realize I just solved the riddle. He bows his head and winks at me.

"So...do you like the gift?" he asks such an obvious question.

"I love it. Both the gift and the gift bearer." I clarify. He gives me a huge smile. He comes closer and says, "But there is just one more thing left." He pulls me to him, sowly slides one of his hands into my hair, and rests the other hand on my face. Our foreheads are touching, and I can hear him breathe. He gently presses his lips to mine. At first, it was just a peck. But then he slowly leans into me, and the kiss deepens. I sink into his kiss and wrap my arms around his neck, pulling him towards me. He tastes like vanilla, which makes it more tempting. It's probably the cake he had. Our breaths become heavy as we keep going at it.

His hand makes its way to my waist, and I clench my fists in his hair. We kiss for about a minute or two when his wristwatch goes off with a sound indicating that the time is up. He looks at his watch and then at me and says, "I gotta go." I nod. Before he leaves, he gives me one last smooch and leaves me alone to my thoughts and his scent.

~~~

I go back down and find Aunt Ivy talking to my mom. "Aunt Ivy? You made it!" I say giving her a hug.

"Aw happy birthday, dear."

"Thanks! But I thought you said you weren't coming."

"Well, I come bearing news. Good news." She sounds happy. I wait for her to reveal the news and she says, "I am divorcing William." I look at her, my mom, then back at her. "Really?"

She nods and says, "Absolutely." I smile and respond with, "Finally. Good got you!"

"Yeah. But did he agree to this?" my mom asks. Aunt Ivy shakes her head. "That's what I thought."

"Well, he can't keep this up for long. Meet up with the lawyer and talk it out asap," my dad comes and adds.

"What is that?" my mom asks, eyeing the box in my hand.

"Oh, it's a gift from Liam."

"Who is Liam? Your boyfriend?" Aunt Ivy questions. I nod and she turns into my best friend.

"Oh, my god! This is so exciting. My baby girl has grown enough to have a boyfriend. I need details later."

"You got it." I say and my mom takes her into the kitchen to talk. I make my way to the bedroom to treasure this gift, but I am interrupted by Kelly.

"L! You wouldn't believe what happened. I heard that Linda slapped Gavin. Twice!" she says with such enthusiasm. I laugh as well because he finally got what he deserved. But I wouldn't say two slaps were nearly enough.

"And...Jeremy asked me out."

"Who's Jeremy?"

"He is in my Spanish class. We've talked but never did I think he would ask me out."

"So, what'd you say?"

"I said maybe."

"Maybe?"

"I don't know." She looks away.

"He is not Gavin if that's what you're worried about."

"I know. I want to give it a try, but..."

"But what?"

"You know, just...trust issues." Makes sense.

"I get it. But c'mon if you want to, you should. This time, you be extra careful and maybe a little less attached for a while. Just until you figure him out." She sighs and shakes her head. "Enough about me. we will discuss my situation later. What's that?" she asks pointing to the gift box. "Did Liam give you that?"

I nod with a hint of a smile and say, "Okay, I gotta tell you something." She senses the vibe and says, "OMG! Did it finally happen?" I answer her with my eyes, and she chortles and exclaims, "Sweet!" I shush her and say, "It was so intense, and he was so—"

"Irresistible?" she finishes my sentence. That is a much better explanation so, I give a dreamy nod. She looks past me and says, "You know what? Am gonna give it a shot with Jeremy." I turn around to look at what she is looking and when I see him, I say, "Yeah, you should."

"I am shooting the shot right now," she says and heads towards him, but she halts mid-way and says, "Oh, and this isn't over. I need the deets," with a wink. I give her a thumbs up and wish her luck. I head back to my room and place the gift in my desk drawer and stick the picture of us on the dressing mirror so that I get to see it every day. I clean up my room for a while and then head back, most of them had already left and a few were about to leave. I don't mind them and head to the kitchen to get a drink. I stop at a distance when I see Uncle William. My parents and Aunt Ivy are trying to talk to him. I can't hear them, so I move to get a little closer. I position myself in a way that I can hear and see them, but they can't see me. "Well, you aren't gonna get your way." I hear Uncle William say. He sounds drunk. Definitely not the best approach. "You don't get to make these choices, Ivy!" he yells. I see my dad step in front and defend her.

My mom says, "William you should stop now. Go home and sober up."

"You! You are the one putting these crappy ideas in her head, huh?" he points to my mom and shouts.

"Shut your damn mouth, Will." My dad reverts.

"Enough is enough. Will go home. I am so sorry, Jamie," Aunt Ivy atones. He is no more an uncle to me.

William scoffs and points his finger from my dad to Aunt Ivy and says, "Wait. Are you two— is that why you are divorcing me?"

He did not just say that. I am disgusted by him.

I look around to make sure no one sees or hears any of this and then, there is a sudden thud. When I look at them again, I see William on the floor and my dad standing in front of him with rage. My dad probably punched him real hard. Serves him right. My mom comforts Aunt Ivy while my dad deals with William. I, on the other hand, make sure I don't get caught eavesdropping, so I make my way back to my room. I lay down on my bed and stare at the ceiling, thinking about all the things that happened today. It sure was a blast. I take my phone and play the video of Liam playing the guitar. That's the best remedy right now.

I wake up from the sound of my phone. It pings for the third time, and I see that it's a text from Kelly. She asks me if we could have a sleepover at her place. I text her back with a thumbs up. I realize I fell asleep for like an hour. So, I go back to see what the situation is. Everyone left. Including Aunt Ivy and William. I hope she didn't go back home with him. I see my dad on the couch, watching television, and my mom gathering all the presents I received today. I go to her to help her. She looks up at me and says, "Great nap, huh?" I nod and take the gifts. "Wow, there are so many," I say looking at all the gifts. "Yeah," my mom agrees.

"I'll take a few to the storage room down at the bakery. There is probably not much space in here." I speak. "And...a lot of things I don't really need right now," I add. My mom helps me to the door and my dad lends me a hand. "You cool, dad?"

He looks at me and titters, "Always. I was wondering if you would swoop in and save the day. But I am glad you didn't." I give him a doubtful look.

"Not the best hiding spot," he clarifies. I shoot the pity look. "But your mom probably didn't see you," he adds.

"Nice punch, by the way," I convey. He laughs and says, "Wasn't enough." And then he sighs. "He is my best friend. And Ivy is your mom's. These two people are important to us. But it's just shattered now and probably can't be fixed."

"I just can't believe he would do that to Aunt Ivy." He nods in agreement. "Yeah, me neither. They were inseparable. At least, we thought they were. Guess we were wrong."

"Well, not everyone can be you and mom," I say. "I am sorry, dad. I know, it's gotta suck." He pats my head and says, "Well, that felt great. Good talk." We both smile. We enter the storage room and see that there are a lot of boxes and looks like we've never unpacked any of them. "Dad, I'll take care of it. You should head upstairs to mom."

"You sure?" I respond with an assuring nod, and he places the gifts on the table. He gives me a quick peck on the head and heads to the door.

"Oh, by the way, dad? I am having a sleepover at Kelly's."

"Will let your mom know. Have fun. And here are the keys to the bakery. Lock up before you leave."

"Sure thing," I say, and he leaves. I make my way to the shelves where the boxes are lined up. I try to clear some space by stacking down a few boxes and in the corner, I find a small metal, chest-type box. I take the box and notice that it's quite old. I try to open it, but it's stuck shut and tight. It makes me more interested in opening it. So, I take a set and figure out ways to get it open. When I finally do, I find a few letters. They are old as well. I take one of them and start reading it.

Mom and Dad,

I am writing this because I am trying to stay sane and not because I want to talk to you guys. You guys didn't care enough to know what my life is like. But am writing it down anyway since I have no other source for letting it all out. You're never gonna get this letter anyway so, I don't care. But the one thing I did want you to know is that, if there is a reason why am not with you, I hope the reason is that you guys are dead. If not, and you guys did actually abandon me, then you guys can rot in hell for all I care.

I also want to let you know that the people who adopted me are the worst ever humans to live on earth. Probably worse than you guys. I believe that they wanted a maid for a lifetime with no incentives. And I was their choice. That's right. Your daughter is no more than a mere maid in an aggressive household. I am treated worse than a maid, to be honest. I have been bearing it all for a long time now and I should because they at least wanted me for something. They chose me. When you didn't. And now am trapped here, with these evil people for good. I blame you for this. Again, I don't know your circumstances, but I just can't help but show my hatred for everything and everyone toward you. I exist because of you two and that was the inception of my pathetic, troubled life. Hell, to be precise. I no longer remember peace because I haven't had it for as long as I've existed.

Oh, my god.

This is my mother's. Should I be reading these? Why are these here, anyway?

Is this considered prying? But I am her daughter. I have the right to know her, don't I?

Now that I have read this one, I want to know more. So, I take the next one and read it.

Mom and Dad,

I found my birth certificate. Guess what, I don't go by the name mentioned on it. My name isn't Sarah. Apparently, the Richard's named me Sarah when they adopted me and that's the official name now. But I don't wish to change it, since everyone knows me by the name Sarah. Besides, the name on the birth certificate is just a painful reminder of you guys and that very name disgusts me. So, I made sure no one ever finds it. No one will ever know the name given to me. The fact that you named me just to leave me, in the end, is unreasonable and pathetic. Now, I have doubts about your existence. You guys might be alive and well, with another child, perhaps. Not that I care. But if that's the case, I hope you guys are happy and I sincerely hope the child is having the best life, unlike me. Given that the child isn't abandoned as well. Or, if you guys are alone and decided to never have another kid, well that's much better since no other child will have to suffer. If either of you is dead, then I wish the other person, a slow and peaceful death. And if both of you are dead, well, you deserve it. I am sorry, but that's how I really feel. If you were in my shoes, you probably would feel the same way. By the way, enough about you guys. It's time to trash the Richards. Oh, I forgot to mention that my adoptive parents are Mr. and Mrs. Richard. These two have probably reserved a seat in hell. The devil himself might take them there. Can't wait for that to happen. How can a human hurt another human? Both physically and emotionally. There is a reason why these two never had a child of their own. I hope they never do.

At first, I somehow was able to bear with every crap they did to me, considering that they put a roof over my head, provided food for me to survive and clothing to wear. But the fact that I have to live in their aid when I am treated like shit is something I can't really digest. At least not anymore. I reached my limit a long time ago and it's just going to keep getting worse here on forth.

I get a text from Kelly asking when I will be there. I text her back.

Me: Sorry, K. Something came up. Am gonna have to take a rain check. Will ttyl.

I continue reading.

I have thought about ending my life a zillion times. But now, all I want is to live a life without any of this pain. Why should I be the one to stop living for something that I am a victim of? If anyone, it should be those filthy humans who should un-live. It is so unfair that deserving people die early while monsters like them get to live a long life. I like to believe that good people who pass away soon, get to have an amazing afterlife in heaven. On the contrary, the others get to have an excruciatingly painful afterlife in hell. It's only fair.

My mom's name is not Sarah?

She made sure no one ever finds out.

I wonder what her birth name is.

What did she do with the birth certificate?

Thoughts run wild in my head. This is bizarre. The tone of this letter suggests a totally different side of my mom. How much she must have been through to write stuff like this. And she probably wrote these when she was about my age or less. I can't fathom what kind of life she had. But judging from the content in this letter and what I heard from Aunty Rose, she must have had a terrible and scathing life, with so many hardships. I go for the next letter.

Mom and Dad,

I cannot believe I am writing this as I am crying my eyes out. It's the day I wish never came. It's bad enough that I hate birthdays for obvious reasons but when they make you feel even downer on a regular basis makes it hard to live. And today, beat my last birthday in being a terrible memory. I am bloody sure my next birthday will beat this birthday with even more horrible memories. I couldn't help but think how it would have been if I were with you guys. At first, all I wanted was, to have a party, a cake, a few friends, and a happy memory. Now, all I want is a peaceful, calm, and happy day, for once. No person should go through what I went through and will go through in the future.

There is a reason why am not detailing any of the horrible things that happened to me. It's because you don't deserve to know any of it. All I want you to know is that I have been suffering and you are the ultimate reason. Just know that I was beaten, threatened, assaulted, and that I am being damaged. Inside and out.

No wonder my mom never mentioned my grandparents. No, scratch that. Am glad she never talked about those knaves. How did she endure all of this and never talked to anyone? Am sure writing it down wasn't as effective. How can my mom be so lively and act as if these dreadful events didn't occur? I feel so heavy in my heart and my eyes hurt from holding back my tears. But I still don't stop. I take the next letter and read it.

Mom and Dad,

It is weird to call someone mom and dad when I don't even know who am referring to. And the people who are here aren't worth being called parents. I was eight when I came into Richard's family. I looked up to them and loved them so much, thinking that they were indeed my parents. But months and years later, I figured it all out. And their way of treating me changed as time flew. Today, I was embarrassed in front of a lot of strangers for absolutely nothing. I was used to her abusing me but in front of other humans? She crossed her line, and I still couldn't do anything to defend myself. Instead, here I am, writing this damn letter, which is certainly not helping. I am treated like human trash and not for any apparent reason. Just because I exist...

I almost crumple the letter. I have never been this furious in my life. I cannot believe this woman has been through worse than hell. It takes everything in me to not go to her and ask her about all this. I want her to vent and let everything out for good. But then, this could stir up her memory and bring back all the terrible things she encountered. I can't seem to let this go.

Is she really happy right now? Or is she faking it for our sake?

Now I know why she was always lenient with me. Never has she so much as nagged me. I was given complete freedom and happiness. Which my mother never really had. My respect and love for them have reached its peak if it's possible. Because I have never had any complaints when it came to my parents. They gave me literally everything I ever wanted and the love they have for me is more than just unconditional. And I feel the same, but right now, it's elevated.

There are only a few letters left. I go ahead and read them as well.

Mom and Dad,

Remember how I wrote about the Richard's not having a child of their own? Well, that's not the case anymore. She found out that she is pregnant, and now, the worst awaits. I already pity that unborn child. Maybe they won't treat the kid the way they treated me since that child would be their own. That's what I am hoping would happen. But from what I know, these people aren't capable of love and care. And if they decide to abandon the child as you guys did, that would be way worse. But the child may go into a happy and loving family, which is most unlikely. Either way, the child is at risk. But I have this urge to keep that kid safe. Maybe because I fear that child's life might be ruined like mine, so I feel a sense of responsibility no matter what kind of future awaits him. I am going to be there for the child, and do the best I can, even if am not a part of this family.

That must be Uncle Simon.

She undoubtedly raised him with all her might. I can see it. But did they mistreat him as well? I read the other letters to find out more.

Mom and Dad,

A baby boy. An adorable, sweet little baby boy. He is so tiny and fragile. His cry is cute yet aching. I cannot believe the evil Richard's made something so divine-like. They don't deserve that precious kid.

I already love that kid. I feel a connection even though he is not my blood. I can't explain this feeling. Like I would do anything for him. I will make sure he lives and grows to be a perfect human. I am happy, after so many days of nightmares and trouble, I finally feel happy after looking at his face. He makes me want to live for him and be a supportive figure to him.

I still pray that these people change for their only son's sake.

P.S. Looking at that baby had me wondering if I was the same. Tiny and fragile. Of course, all babies are like that. But what I can't seem to understand is, how you guys had the heart to leave a baby that was so weak and helpless. Guess I would never know.

For some reason, I think that my mom's birth parents aren't the villain here. What if something did happen to those people? As she said, there is absolutely no way of knowing what happened to them and why she was left alone. But what I do know is that Uncle Simon was and is very lucky to have my mom by his side. I read the next letter.

Mom and Dad,

Mr. Richard is dead. A combination of drunk and drive and car crash. The baby is not more than a year old, and he was already stressed out about the expenses which led him to consume alcohol for a 'stress relief', apparently. It got the best of him and now Simon is fatherless. Not that he was the best father figure. He tried hurting his own son, who was just an infant. Just because the budget didn't work out. I am glad he is dead and am sure Simon would be too if he knew his father like I did. Anyway, he is better off without his drunkard, evil father. But one more problem still lingers. His mother. She hasn't been the best either. As I said, they are incapable of parenting, and it keeps getting worse. Now that Mr. Richard is out of the picture, I am not sure how she is going to handle the situation and most of all, my concern is how she would treat poor Simon. No matter what, I am here for him. That's for sure.

Let's focus on the good things now.

Oh, by the way, the baby is named Simon. If there is one thing they did right, it's that they did was that they chose a good name for him. I like how he makes those baby noises. His little hands and feet. His eyes. I mean, those are the prettiest set of eyes I have ever seen in a human. His cute, pointy little nose. Everything about him is just so perfect, unlike his parents who are the most imperfect and pathetic people to ever exist.

How could someone possibly ever want to hurt an innocent and helpless life like that? I'll never know.

My mother is the most straightforward person I know. And the fact that she had a lot of things bottled up inside her is so shocking. I guess, Uncle Simon was her only hope and future to look forward to, amidst all the horrendous events that happened to her.

Mom and Dad,

I no longer feel anything toward you two. Just saying. Maybe I have made peace with the fact that this is how my life was supposed to be. And now that this is my life, instead of dwelling over it, I decided to take on it. You know, like facing it head-on. But I gotta say it's not going well. One good thing in my life would be Simon. And with Mr. Richard gone, his wife has completely lost it. Just as I anticipated. She is the female version of her husband now. Alcohol is her only company nowadays. She doesn't give a damn about her son. I see her popping sleeping pills at night. Even the alcohol isn't helping with her insomnia. And she is way too troublesome compared to her husband. She never leaves the house and is always wasted. I am afraid to leave Simon alone with her. She is totally capable of harming him now that she can't even control her alcohol cravings. She is an addict and a total nuisance. She messed up a lot. Not gonna get into the details because it will take me more than a night to write it. But she is nearing the stage where she could hurt Simon any day now. If that ever happens, I won't let it slide. I will make sure she pays. For freaking everything. Period.

I go for the next letter which is the last one.

Mom and Dad,

This might be the last letter I am ever going to write. I find no reason to continue this as I have finally found a soul that cares for me. A person I can finally rely on. Someone I can ultimately share my life with. His name is Jamie, and he came into my life like a miracle. This is the first time I feel happy being alive. So, I guess this is a thank you. But this doesn't mean I have forgotten the other crap. That's what made me who I am and that's also the reason why I met Jamie. So, it will never go away even if it brought me good in the end. But enough about that. All I want to talk about is Jamie. All I can think about is Jamie.

Jamie...Jamie...Jamie...

It's like he is a god sent. I bet God looked down at me and thought to himself, "Well, she's deranged enough. Let's reward her," and dropped Jamie down to me like he is an angel. I was filled with a void and darkness. But he came into my life with a vibrant zeal just to revive me back to a normal, worthy life. I lost myself and he brought me back. I had trouble trusting other humans. But he made me believe in humans like him. He is my life saviour. I love him.

He is going to be my constant forever.

The only letter that makes me smile wide. She finally found the right person and I am so glad it's my dad. She deserved it. After all the misery, she found a life full of joy and happiness.

Looking at dad from my mother's perspective is intriguing and sweet. I know my dad is like the perfect man a woman could ever want. But what I just read had me wanting to meet my dad at that specific time and moment. I would love to meet them both from back then and cherish it forever. I gather all the letters to keep them back but as I open the box again, I find another letter. I must have missed it. I draw the last letter and open it.

I did it. I finally did what I had to do. And I have no regrets. Simon can finally live in peace. As can I.

That's it? What does she mean by this? Is this before or after she met my father?

I stare at it in confusion for a while and try to figure it out.

What did she do?

23
Sarah

Way back then...

It was my sixteenth birthday and I wanted to gift myself the one and only thing that I have ever wanted for a long time. Freedom. *Peace.* Not just for me, but for Simon as well. After what she did to him, there is no way I can let her be a part of his life. She was a waste of life anyway. Simon was never really attached to her and was always crying. All the things worked out in my favour.

And her? Well, from the way she was living, it was clear that she was just looking for an easy way out. And I was all the help she needed. She didn't ask for it head-on. She didn't have to. As I said, it was clear. You could say it was a gift to her as well. I was waiting for the right time. Ivy had picked up Simon earlier, so it was just me and Mrs. Richard. She was drunk and unconscious, as always. I went up to the room to pack all my stuff and Simon's. When everything was done, I went into her room and saw the bottle of her sleeping pills on her side table. I grabbed it and went back down to see her still lying face down on the couch. I noticed the decanter still filled with alcohol, on the kitchen counter. Knowing her, she would always go straight for it after she woke up. Or maybe, later in the day. Anyway, she would absolutely finish it. So, I opened the lid, emptied the bottle of her sleeping pills into it, and placed the lid back on it. I looked back at her and for the first time, I pitied her. She chose this life when she could've chosen a very different, and a dignitary life. And now, I got to choose how her life leaves. Better than the way she was living. Plus, she would have passed away doing what she loved. So, that was a good farewell.

When I reached Ivy's, Simon was fast asleep, and I couldn't wake him up. I had asked Ivy to let us stay at her place for the time being. She always agreed. She asked me to live with her forever which was such a heartful offer but I couldn't do that to her. I assured her that I would move out when I found a job and a place for us to live.

~~~

A few days later, I was informed of Mrs. Richard's demise. Finally. They thought she killed herself. Combination of sleeping pills and alcohol lead to an overdose, of course. I had received the insurance money for both since Mr. Richard's was unused. Now that I had enough money, I was able to get a place for me and Simon after a year. I also started a part-time at a café and Simon was sent to a perfect school. As time flew, all the ugly and dreadful memories fades and withered away and all that was left were the new, beautiful ones. I had everything I wanted. For me as well as for Simon. Ivy was in college and used to impart wisdom to me. I learned new things from her without having to go to college. And we were always having fun weekends where the three of us would either hang out or go on outings.

~~~

One weekend, we went to her college for a freshmen year party and there was this band that was playing a piece of outstanding music. The lead vocalist was incredible. His voice, his style, the positive vibe, and everything about him screamed a green flag. There were a lot of girls crushing on him.

"Oh, my god. That guy is so hot." I heard a girl say. "His voice is so healing." The other replied. I looked at him and felt a sense of belonging. Like I was supposed to meet him or something. I have never felt that way before, so I wasn't sure if it was a crush or just me being stupid.

"What is his name?" I asked Ivy.
It was like we were bound to meet, somehow.
"Uh...Jamie something," she replied.
Jamie.

24
Jamie

Back then...

Sarah was due any moment now and we decided to have a room for the baby. We made all the arrangements and changes so that the baby can have a peaceful space. I was still setting up the room and Sarah was with Ivy at her house. I was clearing some of the items from the closet and I found a small metal box that I have never seen before. I opened it and found a few letters. I knew it right away that these belonged to Sarah, because there was this one letter that was open, and I recognized her writing. All that was written was,

I did it. I finally did what I had to do. And I have no regrets. Simon can finally live in peace. As can I.

I had no idea what it meant or what she did. I didn't bother looking at the other letters. It was obviously her personal journal and is none of my business. But I did feel like it had something to do with her parents, from what she had once told me. Maybe she already shared everything she wanted to, and I don't care about our past. But if she wanted to hide these letters, there must be a good reason on her side. I doubled over the letter and shut the box. I thought she might not want anyone to see it, so I went down to the bakery, into the storage room, and placed the box in the very back corner on the top shelf. I stacked up the boxes from our room and organized the shelves. I went back up to clean the room and I got a call from Ivy saying Sarah went into labour and that they are headed to the hospital. I instantly rushed to the hospital and prayed she have a quick and safe delivery.

When I reached, I saw Ivy and William waiting outside. I hurried into the room to see that she was in pain and trying her best. I ran to her and held her hand. She gave me a delighted smile amidst all the pain she was enduring. I responded with a quick peck on her cheek. I was glad I didn't miss it and that I didn't leave her to go through this alone. It hurt me to see her like that. She squeezed my hand and I let her know that I was right there. I kissed her head and whispered, "You got this, baby." I could see her eyes filled with nothing but joy and hope, even though she was in excruciating pain.

And after a long, painful hustle, she was finally here. Those tiny fingers and toes. That beautiful face of hers. Her sweet yet squeaky cry. I could not believe we had her. She was everything we had hoped and longed for. The nurse wrapped her around with a blanket and handed her to me. I have never been so careful, as well as shaky, in my whole life. She was so tiny and limp in my arms and I couldn't help but shed tears. Happy tears, of course. That little human made me a father, a better person to be.

I will love her with all my might and life. I thought.

She was still crying, and I swear, it was the most pleasant and beautiful sound a human could ever make. But I wanted her to stop because I didn't want her to exhaust herself and fall sick or something. I placed her in Sarah's arms who was still sobbing tears of joy as well. There was no sign of tiredness in her although she just went through an unbearable ache. She was totally worn out but was not showing it. I kissed her head again and said, "Thank you so much." All she did was let out a weak laugh with a sigh of relief. Ivy and William came in with curious expressions on their faces. When Ivy saw the baby, she turned into one as well. "Oh, my goodness! She is so precious," she exclaimed with a squeaky voice. She took her in her arms and embraced her. "Hey there, little one. I am your Aunt Ivy." It was turning into a sob vest because she started to weep as well. "Oh, my god. You guys, thank you so much for making me a godmother," she said. "She is just perfect. Unlike you two," she declared. I nodded in agreement because it was true to the point. William held her next. "She has Sarah's eyes," he pointed out.

"Stating the obvious," I said in reply. "It's all her. She's a miniature version of Sarah," I added.

"That's not entirely true, Jamie. She has your brown hair. Right, Sarah?" Ivy said, turning to Sarah but she was asleep. She looked so out of it and slept like a baby. I asked them to leave the room and the nurse took the baby to the room where all the babies were kept. I looked at Sarah and brushed her hair. I tucked her with a blanket and decided to get her and the baby some stuff from home. I requested Ivy to stay with her while I was out. I ran home and packed everything that was needed and headed back to the hospital. On the way, I stopped at a flower shop and bought her favourite flowers. I stepped into the room and saw Sarah awake and feeding our baby. She smiled when she saw me.

"She's having her first meal. Don't miss it," Ivy said and nudged me forward. I stepped ahead with the flowers behind my back and saw her cute little face. She seemed still so I asked if it was normal. "Oh, she just fell asleep," she clarified. I breathed a sigh of relief and saw the nurse taking her back to the baby's room. I looked at Sarah who seemed pretty energetic, so I sat next to her on the bed and handed her the flowers. She took them with a delightful expression and said, "Just what I presumed." I gave her a puzzled look and she added, "Well, every time your hand is behind your back, it's always the lilies." I chuckled and nodded. "Thank you. I love it." She pressed her lips to mine. "I am so happy, Jamie. I mean I always was. But now that she is in the picture, I can't be more grateful and blessed. I finally feel complete." I nodded and rested my forehead on hers. "Took the words right outta my mouth," I said, and we let out a silly laugh. The doctor came in and said, "I am not interrupting anything, am I?" We both shook our heads and I said, "No, doc. Please, come in." He diagnosed her and concluded with, "Well, you are totally fine, Mrs. Brooks. Just need plenty of rest and a healthy diet. And the baby is in perfect shape and health. You can go back in a couple of days."

"Thanks a lot, doctor." We replied.

"Sure thing. So...do we have a name for the baby yet?" he asked.

Sarah looked at me and went, "Do we?"

"It's okay. We'll just call her baby Brooks for now. She is so pretty by the way. Congratulations." He conveyed and left. I turned to Sarah and said, "I think I have a name."

She looked at me with such curiosity and a glow in her eyes.

"What is it?"

I eyed the flowers and said, "Lily."

She beamed like a star and said, "*Lily Brookes*. It's perfect."

25
Lily

Present day

"I am very glad to have known the couple that I have seen for years and gotten inspired. My parents are the definition of love and life. Their relationship is too good to be true yet believable." I speak. "My parents are one of the most adorable couples that I have ever witnessed in my life. I seldom saw them argue or fight. Their love for each other has only grown stronger with each passing year. I can, without a doubt, say that I'm the luckiest daughter in the whole world, to be brought up by a loving pair like you both." I give them both a hug and convey, "Happy wedding anniversary, guys. Love you." They both respond with a kiss on either side of my head. I hear everyone cheer and applaud around us.

I raise my glass. "Oh, and I wish the happy couple who just got married on the same day as my parents' wedding anniversary," I say, pointing toward Simon and Lydia with tremendous joy. "I hope you guys have the same kind of journey in life, like my parents. And Aunt Lydia, you are gorgeous. And I don't mean just today." She sends me an air kiss and I revert with a wink.

They announce the first dance of the married couple and while they do their slow, sweet dance, I go to Liam who is standing near the DJ. He welcomes me with a hug and a quick kiss.

"That was some speech, back there," he admits.

"Right?" I smirk. He whirls me around and offers his hand and says, "I'd be honoured to have a dance with you, Miss Lily."

I let out a laugh and say, "The pleasure is mine, Mister Liam." He takes my hand and escorts me to the dance floor. I see my parents slow-dancing as well. They see us and cheer for us. As we both pose ourselves, the song ends, and the next song begins. And to my astonishment, the song that starts playing is 'Lover' by Taylor Swift. I gaze at him, and he comes closer to my ear and mutters, "I asked the DJ to play our song next."

"*Our* song?" I ask with exhilaration.

He nods and goes, "Is it not?" like it's obvious. I blush and wrap my arms around his neck, resting my head on his chest. He locks his hands around my waist and moves along with me. We stay like that for the entire song, and it feels contented. When the song ends, I look up at him and confess, "I love you." His eyes glow with endearment. He grabs me and puts his mouth on mine. I close my eyes and lean into him with solace and passion. For some reason, this moment feels real and unreal at the same time. When the kiss ends, he pulls away from me enough to see me when he says, "Those three words cannot suffice how much you mean to me. But since there is nothing else to say...I love you too. Always have. Always will."

"Even though I suck at math?" I ask with a snicker. He chortles as well and nods, saying, "Even though you suck at math." I hold him tight and wish the time never passes because this moment is everything I ever envisaged.

Too good to be true, yet believable.

~~~

A *few months later...*

I enter the bakery to find my mom talking to someone over the phone. I pace toward her and by the time I reach her, she hangs up and waves at me. I wave at her and ask, "Who was that?"

"Oh, it was Ivy. Now that she is finally free, she is exploring the world and having the time of her life." My mom breathes a sigh of relief. I was so glad that Aunt Ivy was living her life to the fullest now.

I sit across the counter and say, "Don't you have a date?"

My mother smiles and says, "I know, I am late. Is he mad?"

"Nah, he's chilling," I shrug.

She lets out another sigh and says, "You mean he is playing random tunes with his guitar?"

"Damn right, he is." I nod and snap my finger. When my mother turns and takes off her apron, my gaze falls past my mom, to the storage room, where those letters are. The letters that could bring back the hideous memories. The letters that aren't supposed to be the cause of her unhappiness now. The letters that I should get rid of, for her.

"Will you be okay alone?" my mom's voice interrupts my thoughts. "Aunty Rose had to leave as she was feeling under the weather."

I ensure her and say, "It's almost closing time anyway. I can manage. Don't worry. You should go before dad writes a whole new song." I grin and nudge her toward the front door. She gives me the keys and says, "Thanks, sweetie."

"Have fun! Be sure to come home before midnight." I say with a laugh. She turns to me, chuckles, and throws an air punch. I go back and wear the apron and sit behind the counter. I get a text from Kelly.

Kelly: L!! Guess what? I and Jeremy are officially in a relationship! Yay! Will text you the deets later.

I smile and text her back.

Me: Finally! Can't wait to double-date...

As I finish my text, I hear the bell chime and when I look up, my face lit up.

"What are you doing here?" I ask, grinning.

"I am here for your mom's delicious pastries, of course," Liam admits.

"Oh. Great. Let me get you the fresh ones. Only a few are left. We were gonna eat it ourselves." I say and go into the kitchen. Again, I halt at the sight of the storage room. I snap out of it and take the freshly made butterscotch pastries to Liam. His face enlightens when he sees it and goes, "Your mother is an absolute artisan patisserie," he declares. I agree with a head bob. He takes a bite of it and makes yummy noises. I laugh.

"These tastes divine-like." He goes for another spoonful of the pastry. I lean forward on the counter, rest my chin on my hands and watch him devour his pastry with such desire. When he finishes it, he pays for it and says, "I would die for these, FYI."

"Oh, you don't have to die. You'll get as many as you want for free. So...you don't have to pay either," I say, handing him back the money. He gives me a look of doubt.

"My mother told me not to charge you for anything. Think of it as returning a favour. You know, for tutoring me. And...also for the fact that you are my boyfriend. So, congratulations. You just got yourself a lifetime's worth of free bakery products." I say, throwing my arms in the air. He literally jumps with content and says, "Whoa. Tutoring you finally paid off." I fake glare at him. He grabs my face from across the counter and places a quick peck on both my cheeks. "Just kidding," he mutters and kisses my lips.

"Do you want to hang out?" he asks me as he strokes my hair.

"Yeah, we can watch a movie upstairs. My parents are on a date." I say, tracing his eyelash.

"Wow, that is so enthralling."

"Which one? My parents on a date or us hanging out?" I ask with a smirk. He bats his eyes, and responds with, "Both." I gently flick his forehead and look over his shoulder at the clock.

"Okay, you know what? You can head upstairs and wait for me while I clean and lock up here." I say, untying my apron. He straightens up and replies with, "Sure. I get to pick the movie, though."

"You got it," I say as he leaves.

I wipe the counter and tidy up the kitchen a bit. But before I leave, I go into the storage room and take the box of letters. No matter how much I think about it, I end up with just one conclusion which is to destroy them. I can only think of one way to get rid of it all. So, I open it and grab all the letters. I go back to the kitchen, turn the stove on and burn each and every letter to ashes. Her secret will be safe with me, and I'll be taking this to my grave, making sure no one ever knows of this.

These are bygones and not worth remembering.

As every letter burns with all those horrible and unfair memories, I know for a fact that right now, her life is filled with nothing but sweet and cherishable memories.

Now that her bad days are over, there is no reason for these terrible reminders in her blissful life.

Epilogue

"Doctor Miller! There is a couple heading to the ER due to a car crash. The woman is pregnant, and her husband seems to have lost a lot of blood. He is unconscious," the nurse called for the doctor as they were brought inside, on the stretchers. As the doctor reached the couple, he recognized them and said, "Mrs. Vyas?" in shock. He had been her gynaecologist and they were pretty close.

He looked at Mr. Vyas and said, "Take him to the OR. Stat," to the nurses. As they took him, Mrs. Vyas pleaded with the doctor to save her husband even though she was in so much pain. Little did she know that he was barely breathing. But the doctor tried to be optimistic for her and said, "I will but your condition is getting worse. We need to take care of you and your baby first." Her condition wasn't that good either. She was on the verge of passing out.

Just as he tried to call other doctors, Mrs. Vyas grabbed his hand and said, "S-save her. Save the baby—," in a low voice, as if she knew she wasn't going to make it. The doctor couldn't help but sigh with disbelief. He was saddened. "Prepare the OR. Stat," he called out and squeezed Mrs. Vyas' hand for assurance.

At that, she pulled Doctor Miller closer to her and said something in his ear which made him let out a sad smile and nod at her with an ensuring expression. She was soon taken into the OR and was prepped for the surgery. But before Doctor Miller went into the OR, a nurse approached him and said, "Uh...it's Mr. Vyas. He didn't make it." At that, he didn't respond but looked as if it was somehow his fault that he died. He hardly managed to be nonchalant. The fact that he knew them well, made him weak to the point where he couldn't perform to his utmost ability, even though he tried to. He made sure to calm himself before beginning the surgery and hoped for saving both, the mother, and the child. He *prayed*, per se.

"Both of them should live. No mistakes," he said before beginning. Everyone in the OR looked baffled and unsure of it. "Was she given the spinal anaesthesia?" he asked and the person in charge nodded. "Scalpel," he said. The nurse attended to him with everything while others were given their bits to do. As he was doing the surgery, her blood pressure dropped, and her vitals showed an abnormality. They tried to stabilize it but were nowhere near succeeding. Her heart rate dropped and eventually, stopped. Doctor Miller initiated CPR and everyone else stared at him. "Doc, there is no time we should save the baby," said a nurse. He still didn't stop. He kept performing CPR on her until one of them yelled, "She is *dead!*" He halted and glared at that nurse. Although he knew it, he had to try it, hoping for a miracle. "There is not much time left. We need to save the baby asap," she said.

After all, he was just a doctor, not God.

He was desperate to save the baby so he did everything he could. He can't fail them, not now. He kept his feelings aside and concentrated on bringing the baby into this world.

After a long, hard, and possibly an upsetting surgery, a tiny, squeaky voice crying its lungs out, was heard and everyone in the room sighed with relief and happiness. The doctor held her tiny, crying self and whispered, "Thank you for making it out alive and healthy, sweetheart." He looked at Mrs. Vyas and said, "She is perfect, just as you anticipated. She will live well. Rest in peace, Riya."

A nurse went to Doctor Miller's chamber after putting the baby to sleep and asked, "What do we do with the child, Doc? Doesn't she have any relatives?" He looked up at her and said, "Not that I know of. We need to make sure she gets adopted into a good home. But for the time being, let's keep her here." The nurse gave him a look that made him say, "What is it? Spill."

She took a minute before saying, "I know you are leaving for Australia in a few weeks, but I suggest you take her with you. I mean, you did know the couple for a long time. This baby can get a good home with you."

He smiled, but not in a supporting way. "That child deserves a happy and loving family. I am not sure I can give her that." She nodded with a tight-lipped smile. She looked at the form he was filling out and asked, "Is that her birth certificate?" He nodded. "Is she okay? Did you feed her?" He asked.

"Yes. I gave her the formula. She is sound asleep," the nurse replied.

"Good." She turned to leave but halted. She looked at him and said, "By the way, what did Mrs. Vyas tell you right before she was sent into the OR?"

He didn't look up this time. He answered her just as he wrote the name on the birth certificate...

Alisha Vyas.

CPSIA information can be obtained
at www.ICGtesting.com
Printed in the USA
BVHW032243220623
666253BV00005B/342

9 798889 597476